DIRTY ROTTEN VAMPIRES

Broken Heart Paranormal Mystery Series #1

MICHELE BARDSLEY

Copyright © 2018 by Michele Bardsley

All rights reserved.

No part of this book may be reproduced in any form or by any electronic or mechanical means, including information storage and retrieval systems, without written permission from the author, except for the use of brief quotations in a book review.

Any trademarks, service marks, product names or named features are assumed to be the property of their respective owners, and are used only for reference. There is no implied endorsement from the author of this work.

All characters in this book have no existence outside the imagination of the author, and have no relation whatever to anyone bearing the same name or names. All incidents are pure invention.

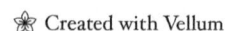

❦ Created with Vellum

To my Viking
I love you always.

To Renee, who is the reason this book was finished.
I love you, BFF!

"*Well, I'll say it again. Demons I get. People are crazy.*"
-*Dean Winchester from "The Benders" on Supernatural*

CHAPTER ONE

The bed-and-breakfast looked less like a welcoming place of rest and respite and more like the setting of a *Murder, She Wrote* episode. Admittedly, my current infatuation with Cabot Cove and Jessica Fletcher was the reason we'd picked Maine for our weekend getaway. But I hadn't expected our accommodations to reach this level of authenticity.

Surrounded by tall, thick-branched spruce trees, the Thompson Twins Bed & Breakfast squatted near the edge of a jagged cliff. Typical of the Cape-Cod style, the two-story house had a steep-pitched, gabled roof. On it perched two rectangular dormer windows spaced an equal distance apart. The bright white accents of the porch and the shutters offered a stark contrast to the dark gray clapboard exterior.

With the incoming thunderstorm roiling across the black evening sky, it was darker than sin outside. I saw fine, however, thanks to my preternatural vision.

Oh, I'm a vampire.

My name is Jessica O'Halloran. I know, right? Jessica Fletcher and Jessica O'Halloran? That the crime-solving heroine's name is Jessica is just another reason I'm enamored of the classic TV show. I got vampified—what our kind calls Turned—when I was thirty-six and I still looked that young. Well, better, because getting Turned smoothed out my wrinkles, perked up my boobs, deleted my stretch marks, added adorable sparkles to my eyes, and made my brown hair shine like polished carnelian.

Those last two details about myself come from my husband, Patrick, who is also a vampire. In fact, he was the reason for my undead status. I mean, he didn't kill me, or anything. A slobbering Bigfoot-type creature attacked me and the only way for Patrick to save my life was to Turn me.

Patrick was 4,000 years older than me.

Given his real age, you might think Patrick was a decrepit Nosferatu-type bloodsucker. My husband looked nothing like the hook-nosed, bald, needs-a-dentist-STAT Count Orlock. In fact, Patrick's appearance was closer to Pierce Brosnan in his Remington Steele days with shoulder-length black hair, muscles on his muscles, and very unusual eyes—a silvery gray color. My hubby had died in his early twenties, so I kinda looked like a cougar who'd married a recent college graduate.

Technically, I was fifty-four-years-old. I'm the mother of three grown children—human, if you were wondering. A couple weeks ago, we'd sent our youngest off to college and officially became empty nesters.

When I met Patrick, I was a widowed housewife with a nine-year-old daughter and fourteen-year-old son. (Patrick and I adopted a two-year-old boy named Rich after his mother died.) I'd spent my days cleaning house, driving kids around, making meals, grocery shopping, and dealing with endless parental insanities.

Our kids were adults now. My oldest boy Bryan worked for a tech company in Tulsa. My daughter was a biologist. With my youngest son starting his freshman year of college at

Oklahoma University, my motherhood duties had been reduced to occasional phone calls and rare visits.

It was strange, this sudden freedom.

I felt like a balloon accidentally released into the sky and floating away from all I knew. I bounced and bobbled along in a terrifying vastness—without direction or purpose.

I couldn't believe my kids were all grown up. *Sniffle*. Rich was 18, Jenny was 25, and Bryan was 30. In my mind they were still *mah babies*, not adults with lives of their own.

But they weren't the only ones to leave Broken Heart, the Oklahoma paranormal community where Patrick and I lived with other supernatural creatures. My closest vampire friends had gone off to new adventures. My brother-in-law, Lorcan, and his wife Eva, were on an extended library tour of the world. If you looked up "book nerds" in the dictionary, you'd see their pictures. My best friend Linda and her husband Stan, who was a doctor of something or another, moved to Denmark to work with a bunch of other science-y vampires.

With my closest friends off living elsewhere and my children gone, I felt out of sorts. As whiny as it sounds, I also felt abandoned. I used the mother's prerogative to worry about her children until the day she died (or, as in my case, after I died). My kids were out in the world without me to protect them. I know, I know. They're grown-ups. I honored my parental duty. I tossed my little birds out of the nest and yelled, "Fly, fly, fly!" But with Rich in college, I'd fallen into this horrible moping mode.

I was having a tough time figuring out what it was like to be me without kids. Sure, I was still a mother. I guess. Well-meaning people kept telling me to turn my attention to other things. Except... I didn't have other things. I tried stuff, like being in charge of a vampire senior citizen program. That didn't work out. The elderly undead are pains-in-thepatootie. They kept running away and hiding in places—like Arkansas.

Anyway.

Some people I knew had hobbies like gardening and scrapbooking and collecting skulls, but I found all that crap boring. Who wants to dig up coffins and poke around dusty old bones? Although grave robbing wasn't as awful as say, commemorating life events on decorated pages with photographs and stickers and calligraphy. Also, I couldn't keep plants alive when I was alive. Shoot. I'd rather steal skulls than plant peonies anyhow. I mean, if I had to pick someone else's idea of a hobby.

Patrick had pitched the idea of a short vacation because he wanted to get me out of the house, out of Broken Heart, and out of my funk.

I had suggested Cabot Cove, Maine.

Because I'm a butthole, I didn't tell him it was fictional.

Because he's amazing, he found a place to lodge called The Cottages of Cabot Cove. Turns out, Cabot Cove isn't a real town, but it is a real inlet in Kennebunkport, Maine. Here's the thing, though. We're vampires. The undead need special accommodations. Not like coffins or anything like that. No. We could sleep in beds, thank you very much. But sunlight wasn't friendly to the undead. And our diet was specialized as you can imagine. Besides, vacations weren't fun when you had to hide your true nature all the time and answer questions like, "Why are you so pale?" and "How come you never eat anything?"

So my amazing hubby found the next best thing for us—a vampire owned-and-operated bed-and-breakfast nestled on Willescane Island. The isle was only accessible by ferry from Mount Desert Island. Yeah. Another island. It was something else to get here, I tell you. We had to take a private plane to

Bangor International Airport because the alternative was making the trip all crated up in a 747's cargo hold.

I'm kidding.

Imagine a vampire going through security at the airport. We're pale. We don't have heartbeats. We're surrounded by the temptations of walking snacks. Ha, ha. No, no. We're not like those bloodsuckers in From Dusk Till Dawn. Sheesh. Quentin Tarantino likes blood more than we do.

Four-thousand-years gives you a lot of time to build wealth. I didn't know how much moola my hubby had, but I think it was enough to buy small countries. So, naturally, we owned a private jet, which got us to Bangor in record time. If we were normal, we might've rented a car to make the drive to the bed-and-breakfast, but we're vampires, so the human version of normal often presented problems. You would not find a vampire couple checking in at Hertz for their economy vehicle if you know what I mean. Patrick made online reservations with a car rental service so that the vehicle waited for us when we arrived.

So. We drove from the Bangor International Airport to the tiny town of Bar Harbor on Mount Desert Island. Then we got onto a ferry so small it could only deliver one car at a time. We chugged three miles across the Atlantic Ocean. After we reached Willescane Island, we'd driven up a steep, narrow road that twisted through the forested hills and ended at the bed-and-breakfast.

Cue the cheerful theme music of *Murder, She Wrote*.

Patrick parked our vehicle in the small gravel lot next to the house. The area was big enough to accommodate about ten cars, and besides ours, I counted another five. I wondered who the other guests were. Given the amount of cars and the number of rooms available, the bed-and-breakfast would be at full capacity.

I studied the bed-and-breakfast through the passenger side window. "It seems creepy."

"Of course, it's creepy. It's almost midnight, and it's getting ready to storm." Irish still tinged my husband's voice, though his Emerald Isle accent had been a lot stronger when we first met. Being married to a Southern girl and living in Oklahoma had dampened the musical lilt. Every now and again, he actually said "y'all."

Thunder boomed and the threatening storm unleashed its fury. The next thing I knew, a ton of rain fell from the sky and tried to pummel our car into the ground.

I turned toward my husband. "We should do the beam-me-up-Scottie thing to avoid the storm." Being a bloodsucker had great perks, including the ability to dissemble your atoms from one place and reassemble 'em in another. Say, from a nice, dry car to a nice, dry lobby.

"We've never actually been inside, so it's unwise to pop in until we get the lay of the land."

He was right. We didn't want to translocate ourselves into a wall or a piece of furniture. Once we saw the place with our own eyes, we'd be able to think about the location and use our transport powers. Until then, we'd have to enter the bed-and-breakfast the old-fashioned way. Like humans.

"This place is only for paranormal people, right?"

"Yes. They host parakind guests although they might have a human or two on staff."

"You mean, as food?" I was only half-joking.

He laughed. "We won't starve, love. But we should keep our fangs to ourselves for now."

Here's the crappy thing about being undead. Vampire-hood took away one of my main joys. Chocolate. Vampires can't eat real food. Which meant I could never try a lobster roll or eat a steaming bowl of clam chowder.

I stared at the sluicing rain. "Whose dumb idea was this, anyway?"

"Yours."

I side-eyed him, and he laughed. Then he leaned over and brushed his lips over mine. The sweet kiss unlocked my shoulders, which made me realize they'd been hunched up from stress I hadn't realized I was carrying. He always knew how to make me feel loved. The simplest gesture often had the greatest impact.

Patrick leaned over from the driver's side and kissed me. "As soon as we get to our room, I'll warm you up right and proper."

"I assume by 'right and proper' you mean we get naked and you do naughty things to me."

"The naughtiest," he promised.

Well, then. I no longer minded the fact I had to run the storm gauntlet. "Let's go, Mr. O'Halloran."

"As you wish."

Aw, I loved it when he quoted *The Princess Bride*. That was our thing. I never tired of the references gleaned from multiple viewings of our favorite movie.

"Wait here, Jess. I'll get the suitcases and then we'll make a run for it."

"You're the best."

He flashed me a grin. He got out of the car and dragged our suitcases from the trunk by himself. As soon he slammed the trunk shut, I darted out of the car.

The rain slashed at us like tiny, freezing knives as we ran to the narrow stone path that led to the bed-and-breakfast's front porch. Mud coated the stones, making them slick, and I uttered curse words approximately 300 times as I tried to keep my feet from going rogue and tossing me into the nearest rose bush. Vampire or not, I wasn't graceful. Still, I avoided falling on my face, and I considered that a win.

Underneath my windbreaker, I wore jeans and a pink T-shirt, none of which protected me from the craptastic weather. By the time we reached the porch, I felt like I'd taken a swim in the ocean. My tennis shoes and socks were soaked. Aw, man. Now, I had squishy feet. My shoulder-length brown hair plastered against my face and neck. Despite the vampire's usual resistance to temperatures—I was dead, after all—I shivered like I was being electrocuted.

Up close, the bed-and-breakfast seemed more cozy and welcoming. Barrel planters filled with a variety of multi-colored flowers sat on either side of the red-painted door. The wide porch held white wicker chairs and tables just big enough to hold a book and a drink. You know, I could imagine sitting out here on a nice fall day sipping tea and reading a mystery novel. I mean, if I were human. Vampires exploded in sunlight. My husband, because he was one of the oldest vampires in the world, could tolerate more light than most of our kind, but not even he would intentionally sit outside on a sunny day. Not that we could. The minute the sun appeared, vampires fell sleep—whether we wanted to or not.

Patrick reached for the front door's handle, but before his fingers touched it, the door opened. A trim female wearing a knee-length black dress with lace fringe and matching flats appeared. Her brunette hair was cut into a bob with finger waves and framed a friendly, heart-shaped face. Like most vampires, her skin was as pale as fresh cream. Her blue eyes sparkled with welcome as she waved us inside.

"It's raining cats and dogs out there," she said as we stepped through the doorway. "You two must be Jessica and Patrick O'Halloran. Welcome to the Thompson Twins Bed and Breakfast."

CHAPTER TWO

I resisted the urge to giggle. On the way here, I'd tortured Patrick with every Thompson Twins song I could remember. I do not have the dulcet tones of Adele, but I have enthusiasm. I spent my teen years in the 1980s and I knew all the songs of my youth, including most of the Thompson Twins songs such as *Hold Me Now*, *Doctor! Doctor!*, and *Lay Your Hands on Me*. I'm sure Patrick loved all the ear worms I'd planted inside his head. If we hadn't been in a car, I would've supplemented my singing with awesome 1980s dance moves—including the robot and moonwalking. I would've broken out Madonna's "Vogue," too. It's a real pleasure being married to me, I tell you.

Patrick plopped our suitcases onto the carpeted foyer.

"I'm Gretta Thompson. My sister, Lilly, is tending to another guest. We have a full house this weekend, which is always fun. Don't you love meeting new people?" Gretta bustled off before we could answer the question and then returned with big, fluffy white towels. While we dried off, Gretta whisked away our suitcases.

The foyer was spacious, painted white with dark blue

accents. To the left of where we stood was a wooden bench that looked hand-carved, and was presumably for people waiting to check into the B&B. Next to the bench was a metal umbrella stand with several colorful umbrellas sticking out of it. On the other side of the bench was a door and since I'm the curious-type, I opened it and took a peek. It was a tiny half-bath with a toilet and sink. Given its size and the modern-day fixtures, I figured it used to be a coat closet. I shut the door and continued to look around.

To our right was the check-in counter. It was probably only five feet in length and held a call bell, an opened sign-in book, a vase of artfully arranged roses and a business card holder filled with the B&B's cards. On the wall behind the counter was a black-and-white photograph of the house. It looked pretty much the same except for the Ford Model T sitting in front of it.

"I had a Tin Lizzie," mused Patrick as he studied the photo. "It was really fun to drive."

I glanced at my husband. Sometimes, I forgot he'd lived many, many lifetimes before he met me. I could see him behind the wheel of the Model T, wind whipping through his shoulder-length hair, his grin wide as he shot down the road. Of course, that's how he looked when he drove modern-day cars with the windows down, too.

Gretta suddenly reappeared behind the counter, reminding me she was a vampire. She moved faster than even my eyes could track. I figured she was careful around the human staff, but with us, she didn't have to worry.

"Are you hungry?" asked Gretta. "We have some bagged blood. Not as appetizing as fresh, of course, but it does the trick."

"Thanks, but we ate before we left," said Patrick.

He doesn't mean we attacked a couple of people in an alleyway and sucked them dry. There's a donor system in place for the modern-day vampire. Some humans know about our kind and volunteer their necks so we can feed. By volunteer, I mean they got payments and other perks for their donations. Vampires didn't need to drain anybody and honestly, trying to imbibe more than a pint didn't really do much more than give a greedy vampire a massive stomachache.

"Tomorrow night, you'll get breakfast delivered right to your room." Gretta took our damp towels. "You two are in our luxury basement suite. Lilly and I have the room across from yours. No windows down there. And it's soundproof. Not that vampires need it." She lowered her voice. "We sleep like the dead."

Her laughter tinkled at her silly joke.

Oh em gee. She was adorable. I very much liked Ms. Gretta Thompson.

"How does the whole parakind and human thing work?" I asked. "If you and your sister sleep all day, who watches out for the guests?"

"Ah. Well, we don't usually host human guests, but we need mortals to fix things around the house or landscape for us. We recently hired a new day manager—Margaret Maple. She's a human widow with no other family. Knows all about parakind, though, so that's a plus. It was fortunate that we found her so quickly. Our previous manager stopped showing up to work a few days ago." She shrugged, as though replacing day managers was something she did often.

"So does she live in Bar Harbor and take the ferry here?" I asked. I found myself fascinated by the inner workings of a paranormal bed-and-breakfast. How did hiring humans work for a place like this?

"Our previous day manager did, but Margaret lives here on the island—in the smaller of the two cottages we have.

But even when she's not working, she's in the parlor crocheting."

Maybe I was channeling Jessica Fletcher, but something Gretta said earlier bugged me. "What you do you mean you don't *usually* host human guests?"

"Ah. Well. We're not sure how it happened, but a man from New York booked a room with us. How a human found our website is a mystery. You know how the Paranormal Network operates, right? It's bespelled so humans don't stumble onto parakind's websites and search engines. You can imagine our surprise when he arrived this evening to check-in. I informed the other paranormal guests right away so we don't give the poor man a heart attack." She looked at us. "Is having a human here a problem for you?"

"Not at all," said Patrick. "Right, Jess?"

"I'm cool with it."

"Wonderful! You're our only vampire guests this weekend. We also have werewolf newlyweds, two witches—mother and daughter, and a root doctor."

"What's a root doctor?" I imagined an individual in a white lab coat applying a stethoscope to a tree root and then sternly saying, "Take two fertilizer tablets and call me in the morning."

"Root doctors make and dispense herbal ointments and potions," said Gretta. "They can also create spells and lift curses."

"So, like a witch doctor then?" This was a wild guess on my part. I didn't know anything about witch doctors, though I had a few friends who were witches. We had all kinds in Broken Heart and generally they were nice folks.

"Ah. Some witches are root doctors, but not all root doctors are witches." Gretta gave her tinkling laugh again. She disappeared for three seconds, reappeared without the damp towels, and then tapped the sign-in book. I noticed

Gretta's silver filigree necklace with its oval-shaped medallion. It shone with four birthstones: two opals, one peridot, and one garnet.

"That's a beautiful necklace," I said.

"Oh." Gretta gripped the medallion and tucked it under her dress. I wondered why she wanted to keep it out of sight. "Thank you. It was my mother's." She smiled. "To check-in, all you have to do is sign the guest registry. I already have your credit card on file—unless there's a different one you'd like to use for additional amenities or other expenses."

"The one on file is fine," said Patrick. He signed us in and put the pen down. I found signing the guestbook a charming way to check in to the B&B. I could tell my husband liked it, too. Don't get me wrong. He adored technology. But we all have emotional anchors that keep us connected to our pasts. Some are pleasant reminders—like hotel guest registries and Thompson Twins songs.

"I'll give you the nickel tour." She pointed to the staircase in front of us. "Up there are four bedrooms. Everyone upstairs shares the guest bathroom. See the hallway to the left of the stairs? If you keep going, you'll find the enclosed sitting porch with rocking chairs, tables, and a couple of bookshelves filled with paperbacks and hardcovers. We also keep pillows and throws out there because it gets chilly fast here. If you want to visit the back garden, go on through the screen porch door. The path takes you straight to the fire pit area, where there's seating for about ten people. From there, you can visit the flower garden or take a meander through our vegetable garden." Gretta gestured for us to follow her and led us through the doorway on the right side of the check-in counter. "Here's the dining room. We serve our continental breakfast in the parlor, but guests eat lunches and dinners in here."

The rectangular cherry wood dining table had enough

room for five straightback chairs on both sides, plus chairs at either end. A large white vase filled with pink and white roses sat on the center of the table. On the right side of the room I saw a buffet with a white lace runner draped over it. Three different tea seats graced its countertop: on the left, a white ceramic with gold-rimmed cups and plates; the middle one was highly polished silver; and the set on the right was pale green ceramic dotted with tiny white flowers. Above the buffet was an oval-shaped mirror set inside an elaborately carved wooden frame. On either side of the mirror were black and white photographs.

The left picture featured an unsmiling man and woman standing in front of the same Model T I'd seen in the foyer's picture. The man wore a dark suit with a silk handkerchief sticking out of his top left pocket. He also wore a fedora pulled down low, which shadowed most of his face. The woman wore a cloche hat on top of her bobbed hair, elbow gloves, long strands of pearls, and an ankle-length dress with a drop waist.

The right picture was that of two little girls picking flowers in a meadow. Behind them was a massive tree. In its center was a wide hollow big enough for me to fit inside. Above the hollow, I saw the deeply carved letters: *L + S 4ever*. I wondered who those two were—and what their story had been. I hoped it had a happy ending.

I found the pictures charming—moments in time framed and left for those who would come after the people in the photos were long gone.

Gretta pointed to a door on the left. "The kitchen's through there. Guests are welcome to go anywhere in the house, except for the basement." She winked at us. "We vampires need our privacy."

"How do you get to the basement?" asked Patrick.

Gretta shook her head. "Oh, my goodness. It would be

nice for you to know how to get to your room, wouldn't it?" She took us out of the dining room, into the foyer, and down the narrow hallway that led to the back porch. Underneath the staircase was the access to the basement stairs.

"It's only about ten steps down. Your room is on the right. Oh, here. Let me give you the key." We followed her to the sign-in desk. On a plaque with several tiny brass hooks were room keys. She grabbed an old-fashioned brass key with a white plastic tag that had #6 printed on it. Patrick accepted the key and stuck it into his back pocket.

"Your bed-and-breakfast is wonderful," I said.

"Thank you. Lilly and I think so, too." Once again, Gretta gestured at us to follow her. "C'mon. I'll introduce you to everyone."

CHAPTER THREE

I clasped Patrick's hand as we trailed behind Gretta.

"I love this place," I whispered.

"Even though it's not Cabot Cove?" he teased.

"It's better than Cabot Cove. We will have so much fun this weekend."

"Yes, we will." His grin told me what kind of fun he had in mind—and that made me grin, too.

I couldn't wait to see what a root doctor looked like and wanted to take a gander at the rest of the guests. As I said before, I'm curious, although my mother always called it being nosy. To-*may*-to. To-*mah*-to.

Gretta ushered us to the left, across the foyer, and into a large room that looked like someone's grandmother had decorated it. Faded rose wallpaper. Big, floral couches and chairs arranged near the oversized stone hearth. Tables filled with flower vases, lamps, and tchotchkes crowded between the seating areas.

On the back wall opposite of the fireplace was a ten-foot long rectangular table covered by a plain white tablecloth.

Most of the huge table was empty, but I figured this was where guests got their continental breakfasts in the morning and their snacks throughout the day. I saw two coffee makers, and a tray filled with sugars, creamers, tea bags, and stir sticks. Next to the coffee makers were two platters filled with freshly baked cookies. I smelled their gooey sweetness, and it made my mouth water. Or it would have if I still had the ability to salivate. Oh, man. I couldn't have a cookie. Not even a little bite. My vampire system would toss out the smallest crumb.

"Good evening, everyone!" chirped Gretta. "This is Patrick and Jessica—all the way from Oklahoma!"

We received friendly waves and smiles, which Patrick and I returned with enthusiasm.

"This is our new day manager, Margaret Maple," said Gretta, pointing to an older lady sitting on the flowered sofa. Ah, one of the humans amongst us. Crowned by tight silvery curls, Margaret Maple's round, wrinkled face was half-covered by her thick, oversized glasses attached to a beaded eyeglass cord. She wore a green muumuu, calf-length cotton socks, and fluffy white bunny slippers. I had to give it to ol' Margaret. She knew how to be comfortable and she didn't care who knew it. In her hands, she held a crochet hook and yarn drawn from the brown-and-gold variegated skein on her lap. I wasn't sure what she was trying to make. A scarf? Maybe.

"Looks like you got caught in the rain, poor dears." Her thick Maine accent made "dears" sounds like "dee-ahs."

"Drowning weather," I said.

"Teeming out there, ayuh," she said, nodding. "Been laury out all week."

I stared at her.

"Your Maine is showing, Margaret," teased Gretta. "We're all from away, remember?"

"Hard to forget," said the older lady. She smiled at us. "But I'm sure you're the finest kind."

I wasn't sure what that meant, either. Was it a compliment? Or was it the same as a Southerner saying, "bless your heart" when they actually meant "you poor little idiot"?

"Teeming means raining and laury out refers to overcast skies," clarified Gretta. "In other words, typical Maine weather for this time of year." She waved to the woman on the opposite side of the couch. "This is Dr. Claire Woodson."

"Hi. Just call me Claire." She held a thick hardback in her lap. I couldn't see the title, but I don't think it was fiction. That size book was reserved for nonfiction—probably some exploration of science or history. She wore yoga pants and an oversized sweatshirt. Her feet were bare, but she'd had a recent pedicure given the pink perfection of her toes. She reminded me a lot of the actress Angelina Jolie—sharp cheekbones, full lips, and intense eyes. She wore her auburn hair long and straight, tucked behind her ears.

"The root doctor," I guessed.

She smiled. "That's me."

"And this," said Gretta as she moved behind the loveseat on the left of the couch, "is our newlywed couple—Caleb and Hannah."

I pegged Caleb and Hannah as werewolves almost immediately. For one, werewolves in lust put out a very earthy sex-in-the-sheets smell and for two, their eyes had a reflective quality I'd only seen with shifters.

Hannah sat on Caleb's lap, giggling as he kissed her neck. Caleb had spiky brown hair while his mate's was long and champagne blonde. They both wore jeans, hoodies, and sneakers. The couple looked young—early twenties, if I had to guess—though it was difficult to tell with shifters. They aged slow and lived for centuries. Given the new-bride shine on the gold ring gracing Hannah's finger, I figured they'd been married about two minutes.

Caleb and Hannah barely glanced in our direction because they were too busy pawing on each other. I could tell that most people in the room were uncomfortable with the couple's public display of affection, but too polite to say anything. Me? I would not spend my evening watching two kids lick each other like lollipops. I kicked Caleb's sneaker hard enough that he looked up at me, frowning. I gave him the knock-that-crap-off-right-now-or-else mom look I'd perfected over the last three decades.

He straightened and slid Hannah off his lap. I bet dollars to donuts that he had a mother who'd raised him to be more circumspect than he was acting right now, and I'd reminded him of that. Irritated that her new hubby had gotten manners, Hannah glared at me. "What's your problem?"

Now, most people might snipe back and turn this situation into a fight, but I like doing the opposite of what's expected because it confuses people. Mom 101. Take the wind of your kids' sails by switching tactics. I smiled at her. "I love your ring," I said. "It's gorgeous."

She blinked. "Oh." Her irritation dropped away as she held out her hand and showed me the simple band with two entwined hearts etched on it. "Caleb made it for me."

"He sounds like a keeper," I said. I winked at Caleb, and he grinned. He put his arm around his new wife and she leaned against him, her smile soft.

I caught Gretta's amused glance and offered a slight shrug. I don't think I could stop myself from mothering strangers. Just because my kids had grown up and gone off into independent lives didn't mean I could stop being a mom. So I guess everyone within three feet of me would be the recipients of my mom-ness until I figured out how to turn off the parental faucet. Humph. I didn't know if that was even possible.

"Let me introduce you to Julia Davenport and her daughter, Serena," said Gretta, nodding toward the two people who occupied the puffy chairs across from the loveseat. In the left one sat the mother, Julia. She wore her dark hair in a short, blunt cut that made her angular face look as sharp and thin as knife blades. Her brown eyes were small and hard, like pebbles, and her lips pursed in a way that suggested she was sucking on a lemon. She wore a black knee-length dress, high heels, and gold jewelry—far too formal for a rainy Friday night at a bed-and-breakfast. In fact, she looked like a corporate executive who should be in a big city high-rise firing people or ruining the careers of her underlings. She gave us a rude once-over. We were deemed unworthy because, without saying a word, she turned to stare at the fire.

Serena offered us a shy smile before looking away. She appeared the exact opposite of her mother. The girl was soft and curvy with long, curly hair and a sweet, round face. Her eyes were blue and held a kindness lacking in her mother's gaze. She wore white pajamas dotted with a colorful cupcake motif and a pair of a white ankle socks. I thought she was sixteen or seventeen years old.

She was also really, *really* pregnant.

Hmm. Close to eight months, if I had to guess. After all, who'd take their daughter on vacation in the ninth month of pregnancy? I watched Serena rub her belly with both hands, and I felt a knot swell in my throat. I remembered what it was like to be that pregnant. Oh, it was the worst. Swollen ankles. Aching back. Peeing all the time. Organs squished by the tiny human rolling around in my womb. Forget finding a way to comfortably sleep or sit or walk. But it was also the best. All that misery was paired with the excitement of knowing that soon, you'd be cuddling that baby. I'd never understood the phrase "my heart almost burst out of my chest" until, as a new mom, I held my firstborn. Because that's how it feels, like your heart is gonna implode from all the love it suddenly holds.

I glanced at Julia and noted her stiff posture and the way her back was slightly turned away from her daughter. I struggled to believe that Julia had been moved by the birth of her own child. And she was not thrilled about being a grandmother. I shared a look with Patrick, and I could see the empathy in his eyes. His gaze rested on Serena's belly, and I knew his thoughts lay with mine. I'd been so busy feeling the empty-nest blues, I had given little thought to Patrick's feelings. He was missing the kids as much as I was, but while I was a Whiny McWhinyPants, he suffered in silence. I took his hand and squeezed it, and he squeezed back.

I love you, Patrick.

I love you, too, darlin'.

Um, yeah, so my husband and I shared telepathy. Projecting thoughts to each other was a vampire-mate perk. Vampires didn't mess around when it came to marriage. Fun fact: If you have sex with a vampire, you were magically bound to him or her for a hundred years. You don't get to sleep with anyone else during that time, either. And there's no divorce.

"Hello!" A woman the mirror image of Gretta entered the room with a tall man who looked like a college professor in his tan pants, pullover sweater, and leather loafers. His skin was the color of dark roast coffee and his hair was cropped close to his scalp. He wore a pair of gold-rimmed glasses that heightened his studious expression. Add a jacket with leather elbow patches, a smoking pipe, and a British accent, and you'd totally have a Clue-esque character: *The Professor in the Library with a Candlestick.*

I turned my gaze to Lilly Thompson. She wore a red dress

similar in style to her sister's, but she'd donned high heels instead of flats. Her hair was cut into a blunt bob with short, straight bangs and sides that angled against her cheeks. Her blue eyes didn't sparkle like her sister's. It was weird, but Lilly and Julia Davenport kinda looked alike, too. Maybe it was the way Lilly's hair made her face look sharper. She held a small, square pillow in her hand, which she brought to Serena.

"Here you go, sweetheart," she said.

Serena leaned forward, allowing Lilly to tuck the pillow behind her back.

"Thank you," said Serena. "That feels so much better."

Lilly smiled. "Let me know if you need anything else." I saw the look of longing that Lilly bestowed on Serena's pregnant belly. There, too, I saw shadows of grief. I wondered what her story was—if she'd had mortal children or if she'd become a vampire before she could become a mother. I was feeling sentimental because *empty nest, don't you know*.

Lilly turned to us. She didn't have the same friendly, open vibe as her sister. She was more serious. And that was okay. Not everyone could be June Cleaver. She crossed to where Patrick and I stood and shook our hands.

"Welcome to our bed-and-breakfast, Jessica and Patrick," she said. She directed our attention to the professorial-looking dude, who now leaned against the fireplace mantle. "This is Duane Cutter."

"Good evening," said Duane in a deep, pleasant voice. My hopes he had a British accent were dashed. He was totally American. Since we'd met the day manager, the root doctor, the witches, and the werewolf newlyweds, I could only assume Mr. Cutter was the unexpected human guest.

"And what do you do, Mr. Cutter?" asked Margaret. She glanced up from her crocheting, fingers and yarn still moving, and smiled at him.

"I'm a writer."

A-ha! So, his professor-like demeanor had been write-on. Get it? Write-on? Man, I crack myself up. "What do you write?" I asked.

Duane looked startled as though he wasn't expecting the question. His gaze flicked around the room before landing on Gretta. "True crime," he said. "Perhaps you've heard of *Murder in the Pretty Place?*"

I shook my head. "Sorry."

"Oh, I have!" Margaret sat up straighter, and put down her crochet. "That book was about the murders of that poor family in Villisca, Iowa." She shuddered. "I know it happened in 1912, but the murders were so awful, I still get the shivers."

"What happened?" I asked.

"The entire family was killed by an unknown ax murder," answered Duane.

A clatter punctuated his sentence. I looked over my shoulder and saw Lilly standing next to the serving table, her wide-eyed gaze on Duane. She held two coffee mugs in her hand that trembled so badly the mugs clinked against each other. "Why are you here, Mr. Cutter?" she asked, her tone suspicious.

"I'm researching my next book." Duane took in her shaken appearance and frowned. "I plan to write about the Willescane murders."

CHAPTER FOUR

*L*illy glanced at her sister and I saw Gretta give a slight shake of her head. I wondered what they silently communicated to each other. No doubt Duane's declaration disturbed them. Since this was Willescane Island, I assumed the murders happened here. I'm a vampire, not prone to fear, but like Margaret, I got the shivers, too.

"True crime? Ugh. Why would anyone write that kind of drivel?" asked Julia, her voice filled with disgust. "Who cares?"

"It made me a national bestseller," said Duane looking down his nose at the witch. "And the book after that, *Murder in the Jazz Land*, put me on the New York Times bestseller list."

Julia rolled her eyes, unimpressed.

"I didn't read that one, dear," said Margaret. "What was it about?"

"The Axeman of New Orleans."

"I'm sensing a theme," I told Duane. "Are all your books about ax killers?"

"One ax killer," said Duane, lifting his index finger. "The

Moore family in Villisca was killed in 1912. The murderer in New Orleans struck down victims in 1918 and 1919."

"You think they were the same person?" I asked.

"I do."

"What's your supposition?" Lilly carefully put down the mugs and turned toward the rest of us, crossing her arms. "That the Axeman of New Orleans murdered the Willescane family?"

"Yes. And he also murdered the Moore family in Iowa."

"Ridiculous," muttered Gretta. She joined her sister at the back table and put her arm around Lilly. Lilly leaned into her twin, obviously upset. If vampires had the ability to cry, I think Lilly would shed tears.

Duane either didn't notice how upset the sisters were about the murder discussion, or he didn't care. He continued, "Gregory Willescane, a low level mobster in the Vinetta crime family, built this house. In 1924, for reasons still unknown, he moved his family from New York to this island." He paused until every person in the room was looking at him in expectation. "In 1926, on a stormy night like this one, Gregory and his family were killed by an intruder wielding an ax." He paused again and then said in a hushed voice, "In fact, the anniversary of their deaths is tomorrow night."

Um, had my vacation turned into a *Murder, She Wrote* episode? It sure felt that way. But it was one thing to watch Jessica Fletcher solve a murder in Cabot Cove in a comfortable forty-five minutes—and quite another to be thrust into the bloody past of the bed-and-breakfast and this island.

"That's so sad," said Serena.

Julia narrowed her eyes at her daughter, and Serena dropped her gaze to the floor. I got that Mom might be upset that her teenaged daughter was pregnant, but c'mon. That kid was probably scared out of her wits and needed supporting, not shaming. *Deep breath, Jess.* What was going on with Julia and Serena was none of my business.

"Was he trying to escape the mob?" asked Margaret. She'd stopped crocheting altogether, immersed in Duane's lurid tale.

The writer shrugged. "I have found nothing in my research that shows he was running away from the Vinettas."

"But wouldn't that make more sense, dear? He angered his bosses, and they sent someone to take out Gregory and his whole family." Margaret shaped her hands into guns. She squinched her face as she mock growled, "'He pulls a knife, you pull a gun. He sends one of yours to the hospital, you send one of his to the morgue! That's the Chicago way.'" She straightened and put her hands down. "*The Untouchables* is one of my favorite movies."

"They weren't from Chicago," said Duane, disdain in his voice. From Duane's annoyed expression, I surmised he wasn't willing to entertain Margaret's supposition. I don't think he liked his theory being questioned, and that kind of arrogance rankled me. Now, I felt the need to defend Margaret. For one, she had a point about the mob committing a hit. And for two, she could quote *The Untouchables*. C'mon. How awesome is that?

"The mob could've killed them," I said. "They could be brutal."

"Mob hits were brutal," agreed Duane, "but involved guns."

"Oh, those mobsters used all sorts of weapons," said Margaret. "When they killed their own, it was to send a message. An ax would do that."

"The mob did not kill the Willescanes," insisted Duane. "My research shows Gregory moved here with the blessings of the Vinettas. In fact, I think he came here at the behest of his bosses."

"Why?" I asked.

"Prohibition. A lot of alcohol was being smuggled in from Canada. This island is a primo spot for that kind of activity."

"So, you're saying the Willescanes were just one of a long line of a serial killer's victims?" I asked skeptically. "Do you have actual evidence that the same person who killed those people in Iowa and Louisiana, also killed this family in Maine?"

"I have evidence enough."

How vague and mysterious of Mr. True Crime. I didn't buy it, and I didn't think anyone else did, either—especially the twins. I imagine they had to have known about the Willescane tragedy when they bought the place. But I understood why they wouldn't want guests to know that tale. Even paranormal vacationers would look askance at staying in a place where people were hacked to death.

"So the island was named after the Willescanes?" asked Claire as she looked over her shoulder at the twins. "Was that before or after they died?"

"Before. Gregory Willescane bought this private island in 1924," said Lilly. Neither she nor her sister seemed happy with the writer's knowledge of the house's past. But now that it was out in the open, the story had to be told. "Gregory moved his entire family here, and they lived in isolation—until their deaths. I don't believe the isle had a name before the Willescane ownership. When my sister and I bought the place, we decided not to change the name."

"The locals won't call it anything else," said Gretta. "Though I wish it didn't have such a grisly history."

"You mean you own the whole island?" I asked.

"Yes," said Gretta. "We own the land, the house—everything."

Amazed, I looked at my husband. Like I mentioned earlier, a vampire who was thousands of years old had plenty of time to get rich. Like, super rich. My husband had squirreled away all kinds of treasures over the millennia, and if he could buy a small country, he could also buy a tiny land mass in the ocean.

Do you want to buy an island, Jess?

Does he know me, or what? I glanced at him and then thought-projected: *I can't believe we can buy islands. And name them whatever we want. Hey! I know what we can get the kids for Christmas.*

He chuckled in my mind. *I think Jenny would like to own one —so she can populate it with zombies.*

That's exactly what she'd do.

We shared a smile.

In our paranormal hometown of Broken Heart, the walking dead popped out of their graves on a regular basis. Jenny had taken an interest in zombies when she was a little girl and she'd brought them home with same regularity other kids brought home stray cats. She'd gotten a degree in biology and now she traveled all over the world as a zombie consultant.

"They never caught the killer?" asked Hannah.

Lilly opened her mouth to answer, but Duane was quicker. "No," he said, "Just like the ax killings in Villisca and New Orleans, the Willescane murders were never solved."

Margaret shook her head sorrowfully. "How tragic."

I'd seen some awful things in my time as a vampire, but even to a bloodsucker like me, a family murdered in their own home seemed particularly heinous. Considering how difficult it was to get to this island, the murderer must've really wanted the Willescanes dead.

"What kind of psychopath kills an entire family with an ax?" I asked. Duane's tale of homicide reminded me that this world was dangerous and filled with creatures and people who enjoyed cruelty and death. It reminded me, too, that while they'd once been safe in Broken Heart's borders, my children lived outside that protection and were subject to the vagaries and whims of those with ill intentions.

"Entire family is not accurate," said Gretta. "The two oldest daughters escaped."

"That's right," said Duane. "They disappeared. Some theories propose that the killer kidnapped them and killed them elsewhere later."

"Why would he do that?" I asked.

All eyes turned to me.

"It's difficult to get here. So the killer really wanted these people dead. Then he—or she—kidnaps two kids and drags them off the island?"

"They were teenagers," repeated Duane. He shrugged. "It's possible they were the killers and left the island on their own."

Margaret gasped. "How horrible!"

"That's speculation," said Lilly. "Nobody knows what happened to them. You shouldn't speak ill of the dead, Duane."

"How do you know they're dead?"

"Because it's the most logical conclusion," said Claire, snapping her book shut. "Maybe they escaped the house, but the murderer tracked them down in the woods and finished the job."

"We had the land surveyed," said Lilly. "Other than the usual wildlife, nothing else was found. Certainly not any evidence of bodies out in the woods."

"What about the graveyard?" asked Duane.

I saw Margaret and Serena shudder. Graveyards didn't creep me out. I used to go with Jenny to the Broken Heart cemetery with the same regularity some people went to the grocery store. It was the zombies, you see. Some of them needed to be de-animated and re-buried for their own good.

You know, not enough working limbs to get around or too decomposed to have any kind of zombie unlife. And a few were still recognizable to our citizens and upset those who'd known the person. Zombies were animated corpses with no souls. But if your dead grandma is wearing her Sunday best and shuffling toward you, you tend to freak out.

Lilly sent Duane a look of censure, but he ignored it. "The Willescanes were buried on the island," he insisted. "There's supposed to be a cemetery on this island."

Gretta said, "There is. About a mile down the road."

"How many people... died?" asked Serena, her voice filled with horrified curiosity.

"There were five victims." Duane held up a hand and counted off his fingers. "Gregory, his wife Betty, their two youngest daughters, and Betty's six-year-old niece who was staying with them for a couple of weeks."

"Were they killed in here?" Hannah's voice shook, and she appeared genuinely afraid. Her gaze skittered around the room like the ax murderer was about to jump out at us. I found her reaction weird for a werewolf. Shifters didn't have squeamish stomachs—and they weren't afraid of much. After all, they were the biggest, baddest things in the room.

"Betty and the girls were asleep—so they died in the bedrooms. But to answer your question, Hannah... yes." Duane paused dramatically again, his gaze sweeping across the room. "Gregory was killed right here." He patted the mantle. "In front of the fireplace."

Hannah gasped and then looked at Caleb. "Why did you bring me here? It's probably haunted!"

Was she being melodramatic on purpose? Werewolves knew the ins and outs of the supernatural, and we all knew that ghosts existed. Nearly every place in Broken Heart was haunted because the paranormal energy of the town attracted ghosts. Now, this house might have spirits, too, but that was no reason to get upset.

"C'mon, Hannah." Caleb stroked his wife's hair as if petting her would calm her down. Then I realized, they were werewolves, so maybe petting her would chill her out.

"Ms. Thompson," Hannah asked Gretta, "are we staying in one of the bedrooms where people were murdered?"

Gretta's expression indicated she did not want to answer that question. Then she nodded. "You're in what was the younger girls bedroom," she admitted. "But we had the house blessed and smudged before opening for business. The Willescane ghosts aren't here."

"Ghosts aren't real," scoffed Duane, reminding us all that he was human and therefore, not privy to what we supernaturals knew to be true.

"Humph. Shows what you know." Hannah pulled on her husband's arm. "There's no way I'm sleeping in the same bed as a bunch of dead girls."

"It's not the same bed," said Lilly, sounding exasperated by Hannah's comments. "Aside from a few odds and ends, this place was empty when we bought it. We replaced all the furniture."

"I don't care." Hannah's lips set into a mutinous line. She crossed her arms. "I'm not sleeping in that room tonight."

CHAPTER FIVE

"You're being utterly ridiculous," said Julia. I bet Julia could shatter glass with the high-pitched sounds coming out of her annoying mouth hole. Can you tell that I didn't like Julia? Because I *really* didn't like Julia. So, it galled me that I agreed with her—Hannah was being ridiculous.

Margaret tsked. "Now, Hannah, dear. Like Duane said, there are no such things as ghosts."

I wondered if Margaret knew ghosts were real and was only trying to keep Hannah calm. Or maybe Margaret only had limited knowledge about parakind and she'd never learned that spirits often hung around on the earthly plane. Humans lived in a reality where science didn't have room for ghosts and vampires and shifters and all the other paranormal creatures hiding in the dark.

It hadn't always been that way.

Ages ago, humans knew about magic and parakind, but there was a point in human history where fear took over. They hunted the monsters and destroyed what they didn't understand. That's when parakind took to the shadows, hiding ourselves from the mortals, and eventually, relegated to mythology and genre fiction.

I looked at Patrick, turning on the ol' vampire-mate telepathy. *I didn't know this place was a murder house.*

I didn't, either, mo chroí.

Mo chroí was Irish Gaelic that meant "my heart." I loved Patrick's endearments. In my head, his Irish accent had more of a pronounced lilt, especially when he "spoke" Gaelic.

Do you think the Willescane family haunts the B&B? I sent the thought to my husband.

I don't know, Patrick's voice whispered in my mind, *but with humans, every unexplained sound or feeling of dread is evidence of the supernatural.*

But that seemed to be true about Hannah, too, and she was a shifter.

"Does anyone want tea or coffee?" asked Gretta. "We have cookies, too."

"Are there oatmeal raisin?" asked Serena. Her voice was cloud soft. The poor girl looked weary beyond measure. God, I wanted to hug her and feed her and tuck blankets around her.

"You don't need cookies," Julia snapped. "You're as big as house already."

Serena's face turned lobster red. She stared down at her belly and sniffled.

"Save those tears for your labor, girl!"

Julia had no patience for Serena's understandable reaction to being called fat. Plus, pregnancy hormones messed with everything. When I was pregnant, I cried at the drop of a hat. Serena sniffled louder, wiping at her cheeks.

Julia snarled at the girl as she demanded, "Knock it off!"

I didn't realize I had moved toward the mother and daughter until I felt Patrick's hand on my shoulder. I eased back, but oh, my God, I wanted to shake some manners into

Julia. I gritted my teeth. I don't know how much longer I could stand to watch that awful woman browbeat her daughter.

"When I was pregnant, I was as big as two houses," I said. "Three, maybe."

Serena blinked up at me and managed a small laugh. "Really?" She wiped away her tears. "It feels like I'm *carrying* a house."

"Sure it does, sweetheart," said Lilly. The hostess went to the table, put two oatmeal raisin cookies onto a small paper plate, and brought it to Serena. I wanted to high-five her.

"You go on now," said Lilly, her voice kind. "Enjoy your treat."

As Serena took a bite of the cookie, I saw Lilly glare at Julia, daring the woman to open her mean mouth. To my surprise, Mommy Dearest rolled her eyes and returned to staring at the fire. Maybe Lilly used a touch of her vampire glamour to make Julia shut up. Did our ability to control the human mind also work on witches? I'd never glamoured a witch, but since they were human, I bet it was easy peasy to do.

"I don't think we should stay here," whispered Hannah.

I only heard her comment because I have excellent supernatural hearing. She sounded scared, and yep, I still found it odd that a werewolf might be afraid of ghosts. When you can shift into a badass animal and rip apart an enemy with teeth and claws why would anything non-corporeal scare you?

"C'mon, babe," Caleb whispered back, his voice cajoling. "We already paid for this whole trip—and there are no refunds. We don't have the money to go somewhere else."

Hannah's lips dropped into a frown. "I don't care. I don't want to stay at this gloomy shithole."

Well, now that was not a fair assessment of this place at all. Hannah's whining wasn't justified, either. Just a few minutes ago, the girl was ramming her tongue down her new husband's throat without a care in the world, but after Duane's ugly little history lesson, she was ready to bolt.

Why?

It made little sense. Maybe something else was bothering Hannah, and she was using the whole ghost thing as an excuse. Then again, maybe she really hated ghosts. I couldn't deny the genuine fear of the girl though.

"Did you see the woods around this place?" Caleb's voice turned coaxing. "We can take a long run tomorrow, just the two of us."

I knew he meant that they could shift and play in the forest for a few hours. The sunshine warming their fur and their paws deep in the fragrant earth as they dashed through the trees. Sometimes, werewolves had all the fun.

"What if it's still raining?" she asked, pouting.

"Then we get to play in the mud."

Hannah seemed cheered by the idea of romping around a muddy forest. The mother in me shuddered as I thought of all that dirt tracking into the house.

"Okay," she conceded. "But I'm creeped out right now." She rubbed her arms as though chilled. "I don't think I can stay in that room."

She said that last sentence louder because it caught the attention of Claire. "Lilly, did anything murderous happen in my room?" the woman asked.

"No, Dr. Woodson," said Lilly. "Your room used to be Betty's sewing room."

"Then I'll stay in Caleb and Hannah's room and they can have mine for the duration of their stay, if that's all right."

"That's kind of you," said Lilly. She looked at the werewolves. "Do you want the new accommodations?"

"Yes." Hanna blew out a relieved breath. She glanced at

Claire, smiling. "Thank you so much." Her entire demeanor changed from petulant to happy.

Margaret yawned. "My goodness. I think I'll call it a night."

"I'll walk you to the cottage," offered Gretta.

"In this storm?" asked Duane. "Do you think that's wise?"

I glanced at Duane. I found it difficult to believe he gave a crap about how Margaret got to her cottage. I think he liked being a know-it-all even when it came to things he didn't actually know.

"We have a golf cart," explained Gretta. "The cottages are about 300 feet away, so it's a short trip. We'll be fine."

"Let me get my things, and we can go." Margaret gathered her yarn into a cloth tote bag and scooted to the edge of the couch.

My husband played the gentleman, holding out his hand to help the elderly woman to her feet.

"Oh, my. Aren't you a strong one?" She patted his bicep, and I swear she batted her lashes at him. Well, I couldn't blame her. Patrick was all kinds of gorgeous. She shuffled around the couch, the long ears of her bunny slippers dragging on the carpet. I was a little worried that she might trip over those things and break a hip.

Gretta guided her out of the room and into the foyer. Then we heard the front door open and close. I wondered if Gretta really had a golf cart—or if that was a fib she told the human because she planned to use vampire magic to take Margaret into her cottage.

Patrick and I slid onto the couch next to Claire. She smiled at me, but she looked pensive, and turned to stare at the fire. With her book closed, I could read the title, which was The History of Herbalism in the Modern World. Wow. I bet it was super riveting. Those kinds of books are what my mom used to call doorstoppers. As in, you put the book against the door to keep it open because you sure weren't gonna read a tome that boring.

I snuggled next to Patrick. Oh, yeah. This was nice. I had to admit that the sounds of the crackling fire and the smoky-sweet scent of the burning logs had a lulling effect on me. Haunted or not, the Thompson Twins Bed and Breakfast offered a warm and welcoming atmosphere. I sighed in contentment. I'm kidding. I can't sigh. Vampires don't use their lungs because we don't breathe.

Gretta returned a few minutes later, then she and Lilly bustled about cleaning and straightening. Gretta hummed under her breath. I took a minute to catch the tune, and the minute I did, I grinned. *Lies* by the Thompson Twins. It tickled me beyond measure to know an actual Thompson Twin, a vampire no less, was humming along to a Thompson Twins song. It made me like Gretta even more.

Apparently tired of leaning against the rocky wall of the hearth, or maybe he didn't want to be within breathing distance of Julia anymore, Duane moved to the only unoccupied chair in the room—a leather wingback canted by the opposite corner of the fireplace. He stretched out his legs and crossed his feet at the ankles. He cut his eyes at Julia, and I swear there was a flash of animosity in his gaze.

Wow. That level of antipathy was reserved for people you knew well enough to hate. Then again, I'd only been in her presence for fifteen minutes, and I disliked Julia Davenport intently.

I glanced at Serena and felt another pull of sympathy. Being raised by such a cold woman must be a hundred kinds of horrible. I felt my heart clench. I couldn't help but try to reach out to the girl.

"Serena, do you have any brothers or sisters?" I asked.

"No," answered Julia. "One child was more than I wanted."

My mouth dropped open. *Witch said what now?* How many times had Julia made it clear to her own daughter that she was not wanted? Oh, my God. I felt Patrick's arm tighten around me and I realized my ire was visible to anyone looking at me. I attempted to calm myself, but man, it was hard to bank my anger. I couldn't comprehend Julia's vile treatment of her daughter.

"For heaven's sake, Julia," said Claire in disgust. "Could you at least pretend to be a decent human being?"

Yes! Go, Claire! I was glad to see the root doctor had spoken up. Not that it did her much good. Julia puffed up in her seat like an angry rattler getting to strike, and I knew she would not take any lip from those she considered her inferiors. Her nature was pure aggression.

"If I wanted your opinion, Dr. Woodson, I would've paid you for it." She pointed a finger at Claire. "So do yourself a favor and shut up."

CHAPTER SIX

*H*aving delivered her hateful barb, Julia smiled in cold triumph. I shared a stunned look with Patrick and then we both, along with everyone else in the room, looked at Claire to see how she'd respond to the witch's vitriol.

Fury flashed in Claire's eyes and her hands curled into fists, which she pressed against the book still on her lap. "You did pay for it," she said in a measured tone.

Claire and Julia knew one another?

"You hired me to take care of Serena and I'm telling you," said Claire, her voice tightening, "the stress you're causing your daughter could complicate her labor."

I looked at the two of them glaring at each other. Yep. They knew each other, all right. Worse, Claire worked for the nightmare in high heels.

"I'm okay, Dr. Woodson," said Serena. She pressed her lips together as though preventing herself for saying anything else, like what we were all thinking: *I'm used to my mother's acrimony and abuse.*

Julia seemed to realize she was making a spectacle of

herself. She shifted in her chair and smoothed out her dress. "Well, this has been fun," she said, her voice sharp as a new razor. Once again, she turned away and looked at the fire.

The entire atmosphere of the room was charged with anxiety and uneasiness. Gretta and Lilly bustled about straightening things that didn't need straightening. Hannah and Caleb looked as though they were ready to leave, but couldn't until Claire was ready to complete the room switchover.

Claire glanced at them and seemed to realize the same thing I had. She took the hint. "I think I'm ready for bed. Hannah and Caleb, would it be all right to trade rooms now?"

"Yes!" Hannah jumped up from the loveseat, unable to contain her eagerness. She glanced at Julia, and I could tell she wasn't enamored of the woman, either. I doubted anyone in this room liked Julia. The witch didn't seem like the type to make nice, much less make friends. Caleb stood up next to his wife, and the two held hands as they waited for Claire.

The root doctor picked up her book and rose to her feet. She glanced at Julia, and I could see dislike flare in her gaze. I wondered if the witch knew how many people in this room looked at her like she was moldy bread. She never moved her gaze from the fire, so I was guessing she didn't give two hoots about our opinions of her.

"Serena, if you need anything, just call," said Claire.

Serena nodded. "I will, Dr. Woodson."

"Good night, everyone," said Claire. She looked at Patrick and I. "It was nice to meet you."

"You, too," I said.

Claire left the parlor with the newlyweds. I heard them chattering as they climbed the stairs.

I wanted to go to our room, too, but I didn't want to leave Serena alone. The girl's expression was full of misery. I tried to convey my empathy with my eyes and a wide smile. What I wanted to do was hug her and tell her everything would be okay.

But that wasn't my right.

And it would be a lie.

Serena finished her second cookie and slid the paper plate onto the small table positioned between the chairs. Lilly swept by and grabbed it, taking a quick second to pat Serena's shoulder. The girl sent the vampire a grateful smile.

"I think I'll turn in, too," said Duane as he got up from the love seat. After that exchange with Julia, I wasn't surprised he was ready to leave. He stretched his arms and yawned, obviously fighting exhaustion. "I have to get in some word count before I go to bed."

"Do you?" asked Julia in a bored tone.

Duane bristled, turning his annoyed gaze to the witch. "Good night to you, too, Mrs. Davenport."

"It's *Miss*," she snapped. She turned her beady eyes on him. "Miss Davenport."

Duane shook his head, his expression full of ire. He looked at Patrick and I and muttered good night again as he passed by the couch.

After he left, Julia said, "What a dreadful man."

Her tone struck me as odd—as though she were commenting from the experience of knowing Duane Cutter rather than hurling an insult because she couldn't stop herself from being hateful. After Serena's comment, I wondered if she knew him before he arrived at the bed-and-breakfast. "Have you and Mr. Cutter known each other long?"

Julia looked at me, her gaze cold as she said, "We don't know each other at all."

I got the instant impression she was lying. I didn't know her from Adam, so why would she lie to me about knowing Duane Cutter? Hmm. Maybe she knew him and told him about the bed-and-breakfast and that's how the human found this place. Then again Julia's dislike of Duane might not be personal. She seemed to dislike everyone. Eh. Probably she didn't know him at all and I was making a big deal outta nothing.

"Are you sure you don't know him, Mother? Mr. Cutter seems familiar," said Serena. "I feel like I've seen him before."

"Maybe on YouTube or Facebook," said Julia. "His terrible books are everywhere." She stared at her daughter. "Not that you read."

"I read a lot," said Serena. "On my phone."

Julia harrumphed and rolled her eyes.

I don't think I'd ever met a woman as mean as Julia Davenport. I realized she enjoyed causing people pain and didn't give a damn about what anyone else thought. I wish there was a way I could help Serena, but I did not understand how. Offer to take her to somewhere safe? I'm sure Julia would call that kidnapping. It broke my heart to know Serena was stuck—old enough to have a baby but too young to have any say about what happened to her or her child.

I wish we could help Serena, I thought-sent to Patrick. *Her mother is the worst.*

She is, he agreed. *I'm not sure what we can do, though, love.*

I don't know, either.

Patrick leaned over kissed the top of my head. I snuggled closer to him, happy to be near him.

I heard the front door swing open allowing in the storm's cacophony. When the door slammed shut, it drew Julia and Serena's attention. They both looked toward the parlor's doorway. Julia frowned, but I saw Serena's expression light up.

Did the girl know who the unexpected visitor was?

"I thought all the guests checked in," said Gretta.

"They have," said Lilly, sounding nonplussed.

The twins hurried into the foyer and a moment later, we heard raised voices.

"She doesn't want this!" A man's determined voice issued the fierce declaration. "Where is she?"

"Evan?" Serena's voice held wonderment as she scooted to the edge of her chair, gripping the armrests as she started to stand up.

"Sit down," hissed her mother.

Serena glanced at the doorway, hope in her blue eyes, but she obeyed Julia and stay seated.

"You can't stop me from seeing her. Get out of the way!"

A young man rushed into the parlor. His short blonde hair dripped with water, and he was drenched from his jacket to his jeans. He wore thick work boots, which tracked mud across the wood floor as he headed toward Serena. Lilly and Gretta appeared in the parlor's doorway, both wringing their hands, unsure what to do.

"You found me," Serena said, excited.

"Damn right I did, babe."

I wondered how the boyfriend figured out where this place was. I glanced at Serena and realized she must've told him. But how had he gotten here? It was still storming like crazy and I couldn't imagine the guy running the ferry would willingly take the kid all the way to Willescane Island.

"Don't you take another step toward her," said Julia as she rose to her feet. For a nanosecond, I saw her eyes flare bright purple.

Uh... what?

Evan stalled his progress even though it was obvious he didn't want to stop. He yelled in frustration as he swayed forward, unable to move his own feet.

I glanced at Patrick. *What is that witch doing?*
Nothing good.

An outrageous scenario popped into my head. Maybe

Serena wasn't Julia's daughter, and she'd kidnapped the pregnant girl, and now Evan had arrived to save the day. Oh, I wish. It was far more likely Julia had whisked Serena away to this out-of-the-way place to keep her from the boy who'd gotten her daughter pregnant.

"There's nothing you can do now. The decision's made," said Julia, her voice colder than the Arctic wind.

"I didn't agree to it," said Evan. "I'm eighteen, and I have a good job. I have a place for us to live. Serena doesn't want to give up our baby."

Julia's eyes flashed purple again. "You are unworthy of my daughter, you human trash. I've had enough of you."

The hairs on my arms stood up as I felt the surrounding air electrify. Julia was drawing power, and I felt the build up of magic as she created a ball of purple light within her hands.

Patrick and I stood up from the couch.

"Stop." Patrick's command startled and then infuriated Julia. The woman enacted her powers with unchallenged arrogance. She didn't care she was in a public space with innocents in the room, including her own pregnant daughter. And she planned to do what? Attack Evan like that was gonna be okay with the rest of us?

The bright purple magic now swirling above her outstretched palm highlighted her angry expression. "Who the hell do you think you are?" she spat at my husband.

"Patrick O'Halloran," he said. "Son of Ruadan."

The mention of Ruadan was enough to jolt her. You see, my husband was the biological son of Ruadan the First. As in, the first vampire ever. Okay. Here's a quick vampire history lesson: Thousands of years ago, Ruadan was a *Sidhe* prince who died in a huge war between two Sidhe factions. Ruadan's grandmother, the dark goddess Morrigu, brought him back to life—well, unlife—and *ta-da*, the first vampire. Later on, Patrick was killed by angry, superstitious villagers (boy, is that a long story), so Ruadan Turned him into a vampire, too.

Yep. I win the weirdest father-in-law award hands down.

Patrick was vampire royalty, and he was one of the strongest of our kind. You did not want him on your bad side. Something Julia had just comprehended. She looked stunned, and I admit I took petty satisfaction in that.

"Release him." Patrick's tone brooked no argument.

When she did nothing, Patrick flashed his fangs at her.

She gritted her teeth, reluctant to obey, but deciding it was better to back down than risk a confrontation with my husband. The swirling ball of light disappeared and then she focused her gaze on the boy. Her eyes flared purple again—and she released the magic binding Evan to the floor.

The second the kid could move, he hurried to his girlfriend and knelt next to her chair. "You don't have to do this, Serena."

"Yes, she does." Julia crossed her arms. "She just turned seventeen. She's not old enough to make legal decisions regarding the baby."

"You might use magic, but you don't have the right to ruin people's lives," said Evan. I studied the earnest young man and yep, pegged him as human through and through. So he knew Julia was a witch, but did he know about other paranormal beings? Like vampires, for instance? I had to give it to him though. He'd risked life and limb to get here. But what was his plan now? Take Serena out in the storm and try to make the trip back to Bar Harbor? That was not a well-thought-out move. But desperation often pushed people to do illogical things.

Julia laughed cruelly. "You're pathetic. You are not taking my daughter anywhere. That child does not belong to either one of you. It will be given to its actual parents the minute it's born."

"She," said Serena, her lips trembling as her eyes filled with tears. "I'm having a girl."

"A daughter?" Evan grinned, thrilled by the news. Obviously he was all in for being a dad. I admired that.

Evan glared at Julia. "I'm not letting anyone take my daughter. Arranging an adoption without my permission—or Serena's—isn't legal."

"You think you'll win against me?" Julia snorted in disbelief. "Better men than you have tried. You need to leave Evan. Now."

"Not without Serena." Evan stood up and defied Julia by helping Serena out of the chair. Evan put a protective arm around his girlfriend and guided her away from her seething mother. I imagine the only reason Mean Mom didn't zap Evan into dust was the vampires in the room. Well, probably Patrick was the one who scared her the most. Even though I could be a badass when warranted.

"My truck's outside," said Evan. "And the ferry's waiting for us. Let's go home."

Serena allowed Evan to move her a few more steps, but she stopped. "This won't work," she said, her voice shaking. "We c-can't be t-together. She'll never allow it."

"Damn right, I won't," said Julia, her voice thick with satisfaction. "And if you try to leave with my daughter, Evan Smith... I'll kill you where you stand."

CHAPTER SEVEN

"Go ahead," snarled Evan as he dared to move Serena further away from her mother. "It's okay, babe. I'll protect you."

Evan had some balls; I'd give him that. But he was also delusional. Hadn't Julia made it clear she'd use her considerable power against him? I didn't know if he was foolish or courageous for what he was doing right now—but I thought Serena was a lot better off with him than with her mother.

Serena looked torn, but I don't think it was because she wanted to stay with her mom. Julia would burn down the earth to find the two lovebirds and steal their joy, and that no doubt made Serena afraid. If Julia wanted to get rid of her problem daughter, letting her go off with Evan would be ideal. I couldn't help but feel like something else was going on here —something bigger than a disappointed mom trying to make sure her daughter didn't ruin her young life by becoming a mother too soon.

"You don't know her," said Serena. I saw the quaking fear in her eyes and ached for the poor girl. What had Julia done to her daughter to inspire that level of terror?

"I don't care what your mother says or does," said Evan, "I won't abandon you or our baby. I love you, Serena."

"I love you, too." She crowded into his embrace and burst into tears. He hugged her.

Julia lifted her hands. The ball of sparkling purple light appeared almost instantly, almost like she'd held it in reserve —removing it from our sight, but not dissipating the magic.

"Don't!" yelled Patrick.

But Julia had reconsidered Patrick's importance, and no longer seemed afraid of him—or the consequences of using lethal magic against a human. That was a big no-no in the parakind world. However, Julia seemed to believe the rules were for other people. Her gaze narrowed as she threw the sizzling magic at Evan.

Patrick zipped in front the kids in time to take the full brunt of the blow. The magic exploded against his chest and he cried out, sinking to his knees, as the purple light washed over him.

"Patrick!" I yelled.

"I'm okay," he managed through gritted teeth. "Give... me a... minute."

I'd had enough of Julia Davenport. In the blink of an eye, I used my vampire speed to put myself between the witch and my husband. "You need a time-out."

She stared at me, and then her lips lifted into a smirk. Another ball of magic appeared above her palm.

I said I could be a badass when it was warranted. And guess what? It was warranted. I haven't mentioned yet that I have a particular butt-kicking skill. In the early days of my vampirehood, I was gifted with two magic-imbued short swords forged by a goddess from fairy gold.

And I wielded them like I was *Xena, Warrior Princess*.

I could call them forth whenever I wanted.

Like now, for instance.

The swords appeared in my hands.

I twirled them both as I glared at Julie. She responded by zinging that the sparkling purple ball straight at my head.

The swords glowed gold as I lifted them and used both blades to slice through her stupid little sorcery orb. It burst outward in a shower of sparks.

"No!" she cried out.

I jumped the five feet that separated us and pushed her against the hearth. Her head pressed against the mantle as I put one blade against her neck and the tip of my other sword against her stomach.

"You're done," I said.

"What do you think will happen now?" Her lips twisted into an unsavory smile. "I'll let my pregnant underage daughter go off with her human boyfriend and live happily-ever-after?"

"Sounds good to me," I said. "So you can leave through the front door or—"

"Or you'll kill me?" She laughed. "Really?"

"We won't kill you," said Patrick from behind me. His fingers brushed my spine and relief flowed through me as I realized he was all right.

Humph. No thanks to the witch at the mercy of my blades.

"But if you don't leave," said Patrick in a scary voice that gave even me the chills, "I'll send you to the World-between-Worlds."

Julia's eyes widened, and I saw real fear enter her gaze. The World-between-Worlds was purgatory for paranormal beings. Few parakind creatures knew how to perform the banishment magic and even if they did, it required a lot of supernatural power. Also, the only person who could get you out of the World-between-Worlds was the person who put you in. Imagine how often that happened. That would be... um, never. You gotta love the whacked-out rules of the paranormal realm, right?

"She can't leave."

I think the voice belonged to Claire, who must've left her room after hearing all the racket Evan had created. But I didn't want to look away from Julia to verify it. I had no doubt the witch was a pro at exploiting weakness and the second I let my guard down, she'd use her magic against us again.

"Oh, she can leave," I said. "Right, Julia?"

"Yes," said Julia. "I'll go."

I studied her face and saw she meant it. Though why she'd capitulate now was suspicious. Did Claire have an unknown power over her? Ha. I doubted it. Not after the way Julia had treated Claire earlier. No, I didn't trust Julia's sudden willingness to leave.

Julia looked at me and said through gritted teeth, "I said I would go."

I didn't see deception in her gaze. Hatred, yes, but she obviously meant it when she said she would leave.

"Great." I moved back and lowered my swords. I used one to point her out of the room. "Don't let the door hit you where the good Lord split you."

Claire, dressed in a terry cloth bathrobe, her hair up in a messy ponytail, stepped further into the parlor. "She can't leave. No one can. The storm is too fierce. There's no way to get to the dock in one piece, much less take the ferry back to Mount Desert Island."

"I don't need your intervention, Dr. Woodson," snapped Julia.

"Don't get me wrong," said Claire. "I'd sooner see lightning strike you than be within three feet of you. You're bad juju, Julia Davenport."

"You should talk," responded Julia. "You don't exactly have a stellar reputation, do you, *Doctor* Woodson?"

Claire pressed her lips together, her expression going blank. "You better worry about yourself, *Miss* Davenport."

"To hell with you all. I'm going to my cottage."

I guess that meant Julia and Serena had the bigger cabin that Gretta had mentioned earlier. The witch squeezed past Patrick and then she swept by her daughter and Evan without so much as a dirty look. Lilly and Gretta stood on either side of the teenagers in a protective stance, but Julia ignored them as if they didn't exist. A few seconds later, we heard the front door whoosh open and then slam so hard it seemed like the whole house shook.

I rolled my eyes. Whatever, Queen Drama. At least she wasn't in the B&B anymore and I gotta tell you, the place already felt lighter and more peaceful without Julia here. Claire was right. The witch was bad juju.

I disappeared my swords and then put my arms around my husband. "Are you sure you're okay?"

"I'm fine, love. It hurt me a little, but that kind of magic would've killed the boy."

"What a nasty piece of work," I said. "I hope she falls off the cliff and gets eaten by sharks."

Patrick laughed. "You have a way with words, *mo chroí*."

"I have a way with other things, too," I whispered.

His lips split into a wide grin.

"Thank you," said Serena. Tears soaked her cheeks. She wiped them away. "Thank you so much."

Patrick and I turned to face the girl.

"Yes," said Evan, keeping his arm tight around Serena's shoulders. "Thank you. C'mon, babe." He kissed his girlfriend's temple and then led her toward the foyer.

"What are you doing?" Claire crossed her arms. "You won't fare any better in this weather."

"She's right." Gretta stepped in front of them. "You must wait until the storm passes." She glanced at Lilly, who had a strange expression on her face. "Isn't that right, sister?"

Huh. Lilly appeared to be in a weird stupor, which she seemed to shake off as she answered her twin's question. "That's right. Do you want to endanger her and the baby?"

My concern echoed Lilly's. I didn't think Serena should go anywhere in this storm, and Evan seemed to realized it would be too risky to drive, much less cross a stretch of ocean, with a near-term pregnant girl.

"Okay," he said. He looked at Lilly and Gretta. "Can we sleep on the couches?"

"You two can stay in my room," said Claire. "You'll be under my protection."

"Thank you," said Gretta. "Serena can share the queen-sized bed with you and we'll bring in a rollaway for Evan." Gretta patted Serena's shoulder. "Don't worry, sweetheart. We'll sort everything out tomorrow."

I noticed she didn't say 'morning.' Mornings were for humans. Vampires were, literally, dead to the world during the day. Why do you think it used to be so easy for vampire hunters to stake us while we lay in our coffins? We don't dream. There's... nothing. Just death. And then suddenly, you're awake.

Creepy, right?

"It's upstairs. First door on the right," said Claire.

"I'll bring you some tea," said Lilly. "Go on now. I'll be right there."

In that moment, Lilly sounded more like Serena's mother than Julia had. I wondered again about Lilly's story—if she'd ever been a mother or if she'd wanted to be a mother, but never got the opportunity. Despite Gretta's open warmth and friendly demeanor, Lilly seemed the more nurturing of the two.

"C'mon, Evan," said Serena. She smiled at us, but I saw the weight of the world in her eyes. "Good night, everyone."

We watched the kids cross the foyer and then I heard the familiar creaking sound as the couple made their way up the stairs. Once we heard the click of their door shutting, I turned to Claire, Gretta and Lilly. "I don't think we can trust Julia to stay put."

"Don't worry," said Claire. "I'll make sure she can't come back in to the main house tonight."

"How are you going to do that?" I asked.

"Root doctor, remember? I carry my herbs with me. A sprinkle of goofer dust and rock salt across the doors and windows will prevent her from returning. It'll do for tonight."

"Don't forget the back porch door," said Gretta. "We need to sprinkle the concoction on its threshold, too."

Claire nodded. "I'll ward the doors too, to be safe."

"Well, that's one problem solved. But we can't let those kids leave tomorrow," I said. "Not without some protection—like a bodyguard or a weapon or an evil-mom repellant."

"Serena's due date is tomorrow," said Claire, worried. "She and Julia checked in yesterday, intending to stay here until Serena went into labor. Julia told me that the adoptive parents would be waiting in Bar Harbor for the infant."

"Wait a minute. She's giving birth here?" I asked. I'd misjudged how far along Serena was in her pregnancy. I figured she had another month at least, but I hadn't counted on Julia dragging her daughter to such a secluded location. It appeared she was trying to ensure her daughter had the least contact possible with the outside world.

"We've already prepared for the birth in their cottage," said Lilly. "No one should be disturbed when the time comes."

Speak for yourself, I thought. *I'm already disturbed.* "Do you know anything about the couple adopting Serena's child?"

"No," said Claire. "Julia's keeping that information to herself." She looked at me, her gaze filled with a mixture of anger and guilt. "I'm a root doctor, but I also have my medical degree. I've delivered more than a dozen babies in home births." She grimaced. "Julia engaged my services to deliver the child. She told me wanted Serena as far away from the public access as possible. I see now she wanted to prevent the father from trying to see his child. But I don't think she counted on Evan's persistence." She paused. "He seems to be a remarkable young man."

I turned to Lilly and Gretta, still unable to believe they'd arranged for a young woman to give birth in this out of the way bed-and-breakfast. It seemed wrong on so many levels. "Is this something you do on the side?" I asked, unable to keep the censure out of my voice. "You know, run some kind of birthing center out of this place?"

CHAPTER EIGHT

Gretta looked at me sharply. "Of course not. This is a special circumstance. We agreed to the home birth because..." She glanced at her sister. "We know what it's like to be in Serena's shoes."

"She means me," said Lilly, her voice raw with emotion. "I went through a similar situation when I was a teenager. Before I was Turned." She shook her head, unwilling to talk about it further.

"There's something I don't understand," said Patrick. "If Serena is a witch, too, why hasn't she used her powers to defend herself against Julia?"

"She doesn't seem as powerful as her mother," said Claire. "Or she's unwilling to tap into her magic and use it against Julia."

"Or maybe she can't. Maybe Julia's somehow stopping her from using her magic." Patrick grimaced. "I wouldn't be surprised if she bound the girl's powers."

"That would make sense." I shook my head. "She seems determined to get rid of Serena's child."

"Yes, she does," mused Claire. "I would think adoption would be Julia's last choice."

"Well, maybe Serena convinced her." But I doubted it. Julia had many ways to ensure Serena never had the baby. For all the outrage and disgust Julia displayed about Serena's pregnancy, she'd still allowed Serena to carry the child to full term. It wasn't for her daughter's sake. So what then? Julia seemed like someone who could coldly exchange her grandchild for cash. Had the witch sold the baby to these so-called adoptive parents? Had she lied to everyone about the adoption? Sweet Grandma Moses. I did not want to think about the uglier alternatives. But here's what I knew now: I refused to mind my own business when it came to Serena Davenport. I wasn't sure yet how I could help her. Only that I would.

"We have to make sure they don't leave," I said. "It's not a good idea for Serena to be wandering around Maine with her boyfriend when she's this close to going into labor. I admire Evan's bravery, but neither one of them are prepared for having that baby."

"I better get the tea made." Lilly seemed shaken by the conversation, and who could blame her? The reminder of her past probably felt like getting jabbed by knives. She left the foyer, going into the dining room. I remembered that Gretta had pointed out the kitchen entrance when we'd been in there earlier.

"I didn't realize that Julia was forcing Serena to give up the baby," said Gretta. "This whole thing is just terrible."

"It sickens me to be part of it," said Claire. "But I won't let Serena do this on her own. And I don't think Julia should be anywhere near her daughter."

Boy, I agreed with her there. "I don't know how we're supposed to stop her from taking her daughter. Serena's underage and Julia is her legal guardian."

"If I have to, I'll call this territory's magistrate," said Claire. She glanced at Gretta. "Do you know who that is?"

"Andrew Williamson."

"What's a magistrate?" I asked.

"Magistrates are the enforcers of magical law," said Patrick. He looked at me and smiled. "Like Judge Dredd, but for parakind."

"Oh. Wow. So there's like one guy for a whole territory?" I asked.

"In Mr. Williamson's case," said Gretta. "His territory is Maine, New Brunswick, Prince Edward Island, and Nova Scotia."

"He polices Canada, too?"

"Parakind creates different borders based on magical usage and supernatural populations," said Patrick.

"Huh." It was different in Broken Heart. We policed ourselves. Our little Oklahoma town had turned into an ever-growing sanctuary for paranormal beings. I knew there were villages in Europe for parakind, but most supernatural folks lived among humans.

Lilly returned with a pot of tea and cups on a tray.

"I'll say good night," said Claire and made her way up the stairs.

I could only imagine how frightened Serena felt right now. I didn't think Julia would leave her kid alone. She wanted to make sure Serena's baby was taken in by the adoptive parents or whoever. It seemed strange that she hadn't forced Serena to take other measures the second she knew her daughter was pregnant. Maybe she had tried, and Serena refused. It was hard to say. And all that hatred for Evan because he was a human? Witches were human, too, but with they had the ability to wield magic. Calling Serena and Evan's child a half-breed made no sense. Then again, Julia's whole nasty personality didn't make sense.

Claire's involvement with this whole situation had been a surprise. Talk about keeping information close to the vest. I wondered why Claire was the only one to leave her room to see what was going on. Neither Duane nor the newlyweds had made an appearance. Speaking of Duane, I had another question on my mind. I turned to Gretta. "Was this really the former residence of Gregory Willescane and his family?"

Gretta's expression shuttered. "Yes." She looked at my face and answered my question before I could ask it. "And yes, an unknown intruder murdered them—with an ax. Believe me, if Lilly and I had known Duane's true intent to dredge up the past, we would've never booked him the room." Her gaze took on a haunted look. "Some stories should never be told."

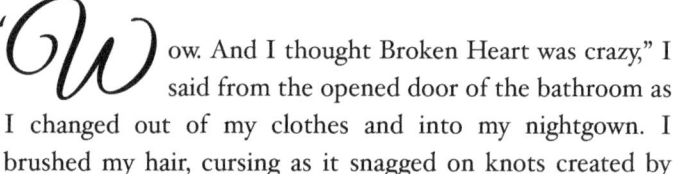

"Wow. And I thought Broken Heart was crazy," I said from the opened door of the bathroom as I changed out of my clothes and into my nightgown. I brushed my hair, cursing as it snagged on knots created by the rain. "I feel like we're trapped in a daytime soap opera."

"Who knew a bed-and-breakfast in Maine would be this exciting?" Patrick had stripped to his underwear and lay on the queen-sized bed, scrolling through the news on his Kindle. Like the rest of the bed-and-breakfast, our room had the grandma-decorated-this-room style, which made it old-fashioned, but also super comfortable. The large basement suite was decorated in pale blues and light browns. A thick handmade quilt and several big, fluffy pillows covered the bed. On either side of it were two nightstands, each with its own small blue-shaded lamp. The large dresser was on the wall opposite of the bed. A flat screen 50-inch television sat on top. Instead of a closet, we had an armoire with a mirrored door.

The bathroom was large with a garden tub, a separate enclosed shower, a double sink, and a toilet. Vampires didn't need toilets because dead people don't pee. Or poop. I'm sure you wanted to know that, right?

The colors in here were variations of beige except for the huge framed picture of pink roses that hung above the toilet. By the way, I can see myself fine in the mirror. One of the vampire myths says if you don't have a soul, you can't see yourself in the mirror. Well, I had a soul. But there were some vampires, known as the *droch fola*, who were soulless, mean bastards. They didn't abide by the rules of civilized vampire society. If you're human, I recommend you stay away from them or you'll end up dinner—and then you'll end up dead.

I exited the bathroom and crawled onto the bed next to my husband. Patrick put his Kindle onto the nightstand and then his gaze dropped to the sheer white nightie. "Why did you bother to put that on?" he asked.

"So you can take it off. You gotta work for all this," I said primly as I drew my hand down my side.

His grin made me tingle all the way to my toes.

I'd barely opened my eyes when there was a knock on the door.

"I'll get it," said Patrick, heaving himself out of bed.

"You might want to put some pants on," I said, "unless you want to show whoever's at the door the family jewels."

Patrick smirked at me over his shoulder. "Just a minute," he called out as he pulled on his underwear and then his jeans.

I got out of bed, grabbed a T-shirt, sweats, and undies

from the dresser, and went into the bathroom. When I finished putting on my clothes and returned to the room, a middle-aged couple stood there waiting.

"Darlin', this is Joe and Mary Harrison," said Patrick.

"We're your breakfast," said Mary cheerfully, her Maine accent as thick as Margaret's had been. "My husband is known as Caffeine Joe—drinks coffee likes it going out of style. You'll get all kinds of French Roast goodness sipping on him." She put her hands on her round hips. "I'm more of a donut girl myself. Ate Krispy Kremes all evening."

"Dibs!" I yelled.

Mary and Joe laughed.

"Well, my goodness." Mary sat on the bed and canted her head. "C'mon, honey."

You probably didn't know blood could have flavors. Yes, there was always that undercurrent of rusty tang—like you were licking a razor blade. But here's a neat trick. Humans could flavor their blood based on what they consumed. I was a donut girl, too, and I loved Krispy Kremes almost more than I loved Patrick. Okay, maybe not. But it was a close tie in the affection department.

After Patrick and I dined—switching necks halfway through—we bid Joe and Mary goodbye. It sounds weird, but we tipped them like we would a waiter delivering room service.

"Sometimes, being a vampire is still really weird," I said.

"I'm over four-thousand-years-old," said Patrick, "and I think that, too."

After we got cleaned up and tucked into comfy clothes—T-shirts, jeans, and sneakers—we headed to the parlor.

We found almost everyone there. Including Serena and Evan. Julia was not there, and I wondered what had happened while we were asleep. I hoped that the witch had woken up, driven her car to the ferry, and fell into the ocean. And that sharks feasted on her.

Sometimes, I am a mean person.

Serena and Evan sat on the loveseat, holding hands and making goo-goo eyes at each other. As young as they were, and believe me I didn't think life would be easy for them, it still warmed my heart to see them together. I had to believe Serena had a better chance at a happy life with Evan than she would with her mother. I had a feeling that girl had lived in hell thanks to her "momster". As for the adoptive parents? I wondered what would happen with them if Serena and Evan escaped Julia's maniacal grasp?

Margaret sat in the chair nearest the fireplace crocheting. She appeared so content making whatever-it-was. I think it might've been a scarf. I had this sudden, weird urge to learn how to crochet. I wanted to make things, too. Hats and scarves and blankets. Things I could give people to keep them happy and warm and safe.

Like Jenny.

And Bryan.

And Rich.

God, I missed my kids.

I didn't see Gretta or Claire. Lilly was straightening items around the parlor. She held a duster and was twirling it between all the little knick-knacks that crowded the tables and the fireplace mantle.

Margaret looked at us from across the room and smiled. "How are you two?" she asked. Her gaze moved to Evan and Serena. "I hear there was a ruckus last night."

CHAPTER NINE

I looked at Margaret and wondered how much she knew. Had the twins told her the full story? Or given her the human version they conveyed to Duane?

"Julia seems the type to always cause a ruckus," said Duane. He sat in the chair next to Margaret. He was stretched out with his feet on an ottoman typing away on the MacBook perched on his lap desk. "I am surprised she left her daughter here alone."

"I'm not alone," said Serena. "I have Evan." She rubbed her belly. "And soon, we'll have our little girl, too." She glanced at Duane. "Are you sure we've never met? Or that you don't know my mom?"

Duane shook his head, keeping his attention on his laptop.

"I think you'll do just fine, dear," said Margaret, offering a grandmotherly smile. "I wish you both all the luck in the world."

Duane stopped typing, slid his glasses down his nose, and looked at the young couple. "You'll need a lot more than luck to make it with a new baby."

His snide tone rankled me. What was his deal? Had he decided to take over being a jerkface since Julia wasn't here to poison the atmosphere? Serena and Evan didn't need a total stranger to judge their situation and make them feel bad. We all knew the odds were stacked against the kids. Sheesh. "I didn't know you were a father," I said.

Duane glanced at me. "I'm not."

"Oh. But you're married?"

He shook his head.

"Then what do you know?"

His mouth dropped open, and I stared him down. I guess few people challenged his arrogance, but I didn't care who he was. He could take his negative attitude and shove it where the sun didn't shine.

Duane wisely said nothing else and went back to typing.

Caleb and Hannah sat on the couch, but they didn't look happy. In fact, there was about a foot of space between them. Caleb kept looking at his bride, but she was ignoring him by focusing on her phone. Had they gone for the run Caleb had promised? Clearly, they'd gotten into some kind of argument because Hannah was giving her hubby the cold shoulder.

Behind us, Lilly had turned in her duster for clearing away empties and leftover food from the back table.

I approached Lilly. "Where are Claire and Gretta?"

She frowned. "I'm not sure where Claire has gotten to." She lowered her voice. "Gretta's transporting Joe and Mary back to their home on Bar Harbor."

"They didn't take the ferry?"

"The ferry isn't running."

Crap. "So Julia is still on the island?"

"Her car is here," answered Lilly, her eyes going to Serena, "but Julia is gone. We checked her cottage first thing—she wasn't there." She shrugged. "She probably used her magic to translocate."

I didn't know witches could translocate. I thought that was only a vampire perk. And not all vampires could do it. You had to get a couple hundred years under your belt before you had enough bloodsucker mojo to transport yourself. Unless you were married to an ancient bloodsucker and got some of his mojo like I had. I looked at Patrick. *You think Julia could magic herself to the mainland in that storm last night?*

He shrugged. *If she can transport herself, she probably left this morning.*

That makes little sense. It's more likely she would've tried to swoop in here, grab Serena, and then leave.

Maybe, said Patrick's voice in my head, *but she might've decided she was better off without having a pregnant teenaged daughter to worry about anymore.*

He had a point. Julia seemed selfish and cold-hearted. She might've decided to write-off her kid and move on. But I didn't think so. Foreboding boiled in my gut like rotten stew.

"Did she pack her suitcase?" I asked Lilly. Curiosity might kill a cat, but almost nothing killed a vampire. What did it hurt to be a teensy weensy bit nosy?

Lilly paused and her eyes widened. "No. The suitcases were stacked in the closet. In fact... the beds were still made."

"So, you're saying Julia is gone, but her car and all of her things are still here?"

"Yes," said Lilly. "If she got off the island, she probably doesn't plan to be gone long."

"Maybe she went to the magistrate," said Patrick.

"Wait. You think she'd go to the authorities to re-assert control over her daughter?"

"I don't think that woman intends to leave her daughter alone on this island," replied Patrick. "And if she can manage it, she'll have Evan arrested."

"If she did that," said Lilly, "I'd think they'd be here by now."

"Only if the magistrate thought she was in the right," I said. "Maybe he thinks what we do—that's she dangerous for her daughter."

Lilly's expression grew worried. "This whole thing is a terrible mess." She grabbed the tray filled with dirty mugs and used paper plates and bustled by us, anxiety rolling off her in waves.

Lilly seemed upset about the situation, and I empathized with her plight. She was correct. This whole thing was a mess. I knew Evan and Serena must've listened to Claire if they were still here. But what had the other non-vampires had been doing all day?

And where the heck was Claire?

Apparently Gretta had delivered Joe and Mary safe and sound to Bar Harbor because she came into the parlor carrying a teapot. She put it on a tray, which she then filled with empty mugs, a container of sugar cubes, and a creamer jug. She walked around offering the beverage to the guests. When she finished, she returned everything to the serving table and then turned to us, smiling.

"You doing okay?" she asked.

"Doing great," I said. "Thanks for breakfast. They were —" I glanced at Margaret and Duane, stopped myself and backtracked. "It was delicious."

"Joe and Mary are two of our favorite donors," whispered Gretta. "They are such a delight."

And tasty, too, but I thought better of saying it out loud. Human ears and all that.

"Lilly said the ferry wasn't running," I said, still keeping my voice low.

Gretta's gaze flicked over to Evan. She leaned in and whispered, "Apparently our knight in shining armor stole it. He broke in, put his truck on it, and piloted it all by himself to the island."

"No way."

Gretta nodded. "Hal Windor—he's the one who owns the ferry—called tonight and told us he'd found the ferry next to our dock. I told him we didn't know how it got there." She gave us a sheepish look. "After Evan told me what he did, I couldn't turn the kid in. Not after everything he went through to get to Serena. That kind of loyalty and love is rare."

"True story," I said.

"By the time Hal figured out where the ferry was, it was too late to do much. He said the engine was flooded. He won't be able to fix it until Monday. Something about getting the right parts."

"Does he have a back-up ferry?"

"No. He has a boat we can use to transport the guests back to Mount Desert Island, but not their cars." She twisted her hands as worry entered her gaze. "And typical Maine—another storm is supposed to roll in later on tonight. The wind's already picking up."

Ugh. That wasn't good news.

"Stop it, Caleb!" Hannah stood up and slapped her phone against her hip. "I don't care that our stupid trip to this stupid place is non-refundable. I want to go home!" She glared at him. "And don't tell me what I heard was just the wind. It was them. The little girls. Screaming." She stomped out of the parlor.

Caleb got to his feet, his face turning red. "Sorry, everyone. I don't know why, but the whole haunted house idea has her upset. She couldn't sleep at all last night and kept saying she heard the little girls crying and yelling." He shrugged. "I didn't hear anything, but I checked outside anyway. I figured it was an animal yowling or something."

"You're probably right," said Gretta. "We have a lot of wildlife on the island. She no doubt heard the nocturnal animals making noises." She nodded toward the doorway where Hannah had exited. We heard the front door slam. "Go after her. It's windy and muddy out there, and it's supposed to rain again soon."

"It's dark, too. The outside lights aren't working," said Lilly.

"Did the bulbs burn out?" asked Patrick, frowning.

"Our electricity is wonky," said Gretta. "It's a constant problem in this old house. Every time we fix one thing, another thing goes out."

"You want me to look at it?" asked my husband. No matter how old or what species a male was they always looked to fix the problems around them.

"Oh, no," said Gretta, waving her hands as though shooing away his suggestion. "We have an electrician who knows this house inside and out. I'm sure he'll have whatever-it-is straightened out in no time flat."

"If you're sure," said Patrick.

"Absolutely." Gretta ushered us toward the couch that Caleb and Hannah had abandoned. "You two sit down and relax. This is your vacation. Now, we have magazines and board games. How about a rousing game of Candyland?" Gretta's laughter tinkled.

"I'm in," I said. I looked at my husband. "I'm gonna whoop your cute butt."

"We'll see about that, love."

Gretta hustled off to grab the game as Patrick and I sat down. She returned and placed the cardboard box on the coffee table in front of the couch. I popped off the lid and removed the playing pieces and cards.

I heard the front door open again and then crashing footsteps against the hardwood floors. Caleb and Hannah rushed into the parlor, breathing heavy as though they'd been running hard. They looked wide-eyed and scared.

The panic on their faces had Patrick and I leaping up from the couch. "What's wrong?" I asked.

"She's dead," whispered Hannah, her face white.

"Who's dead?" asked Patrick.

Caleb swallowed hard. "Julia Davenport."

CHAPTER TEN

"My mom is *dead?*" Serena scooted to the edge of the love seat as if she intended to stand up. But Evan put his arm around his girlfriend, for comfort, no doubt, but also to keep her seated. She started weeping. As awful as Julia had been to Serena, it still had to be a shock to know her mother had died.

My heart hurt for the girl.

"I'm sorry," said Caleb, his expression regretful as he looked at Serena. But she didn't hear him. How could she? Sobs shook her whole body.

"Where?" asked Gretta.

"On the side of the house." Hannah swayed. "I tripped over her."

I heard Margaret's gasp. Duane closed his computer, got up from his chair, and put the MacBook down where he'd been sitting. "Do you have flashlights?"

"I'll get Gretta," said Lilly. She hurried into another part of the house and returned a minute later with three large flashlights. She handed one to Patrick and one to Duane.

"Let's go." She paused. "Lilly, you better call the—uh, authorities."

She probably meant the magistrate. I doubted they wanted human police poking around the island and asking questions about the guests. Especially a dead guest. Or undead guests.

Lilly nodded, worry furrowing her brow.

Margaret put down her crochet and went to Hannah, leading the girl to the couch. She sat down with her. Hannah leaned into Margaret and accepted the woman's comfort. "Now, now," she said, stroking the girl's hair, "everything will be all right."

I didn't believe that for a second. Everything would not be all right because Julia was dead. I mean, maybe she left last night, slipped in the mud, and fatally hit her head. But the ugly feeling that slid into my stomach like rancid grease told me otherwise. What I couldn't understand was if Julia's body was outside where the werewolves tripped over it—why didn't anyone tooling around during the day find her first?

And again—where had Claire gotten to?

As if me thinking her name made her appear, she stepped into the parlor. She wore a pair of pink sweats and her hair was wrapped in a towel. It was obvious she'd just come from a shower. I guess that answered the question about where'd she been all this time. "What's going on?"

"Caleb and Hannah found Julia," I said. "She's dead."

Surprise flashed across her face. "Where is she?"

"On the side of the house," said Caleb.

"You'd better see to Serena," I told Claire. "She's upset."

Claire nodded and crossed the parlor to check on the crying girl. I watched her squat down next to Serena and pat her arm, trying to soothe her. I don't know what she said, but Serena made a visible effort to staunch the flow of her tears.

We followed Duane outside. Vampires and werewolves

didn't need flashlights to see in the dark, but humans did. Duane had appointed himself the leader of the body brigade, and he turned on his flashlight, so we turned on ours, too.

Caleb led us off the porch and onto the narrow stone path I nearly slipped off last night. Given how many times I'd nearly lost my footing, I could believe that Julia might've taken herself out by losing her balance and breaking her neck.

And then what? Rolled her own dead body off the path and onto the side of the house?

Yeah, right.

The path wound between the parking area and the left side of the house. Tall, well-trimmed bushes blocked the lot from view. There wasn't too much room between those hedges and the side of the house. We had to walk in single file with Caleb leading the way and Duane behind him, followed by Patrick, me, and Gretta. With the rain keeping most folks indoors and how far down she was on the narrow and secluded path, I could see why no one had discovered Julia before now.

"What were you doing out here?" asked Duane. His tone had a stern investigatory tone.

"Hannah ran off," said Caleb. "I followed her, trying to get her to calm down." He looked over his shoulder and said, "That story you told about the Willescane murders freaked her out."

"The truth requires fortitude," said Duane. "The facts often lead down dark roads."

"Thank you, Dr. Phil," I muttered.

Above us, the crescent moon slashed the night like a shiny white scythe. As Gretta had predicated, the storm was on its way. I looked at thick, gray clouds gathering in the distance and knew we were in for another rain bashing. My sneakers squished as we followed Caleb further along the house.

Finally, he stopped. "There," he said, pointing down. "I

thought—well, I thought at first it was Lilly. But we'd just seen her inside. After a closer look, I recognized Julia."

Duane shone the light at the area the werewolf pointed at.

With her short hair and black dress, I could see how someone might mistake Julia for Lilly—at a distance. It curled my stomach to think the killer might've been after Lilly.

I shook my head, not believing it. Julia hadn't endeared herself to anyone here. Nearly everyone at the bed-and-breakfast could've wanted her dead. Hadn't even I said as much last night?

The witch lay on the ground, her eyes clouded and her mouth opened in what looked like a terrified scream. She was covered in mud, but as Duane moved the beam of light over her body, we could see the slash marks across her chest and abdomen. Her expensive dress was in tatters.

Duane inhaled a shocked breath. "Did an animal do this to her?" he asked, his voice trembling. The beam hit Julia's bare feet, which were scratched and dirty. Her high heels were gone.

"She must've been running away," I said. "I bet she chucked her shoes and booked it."

"So you think it was an animal attack?" asked Duane.

"I don't know," I said.

Duane crouched down and reached out toward Julia's face.

"Don't do that," I warned. "I'm not a cop, but I know you're not supposed to touch the body." You'd think Mr. True Crime would know that, too. He wrote about murder. Surely, he'd learned the basics from the investigations he'd written about for his books.

"I thought I should close her eyes," he muttered, rising unsteadily to his feet. "Poor Julia."

Yeah, I wasn't hypocritical enough to say something I didn't mean like, "It's such a shame." Because... well, was it? A shame? I dunno. Okay, okay. I know I said that I hoped she fell off a cliff and got eaten by sharks, but I didn't actually hadn't expected to find her murdered body the next night. I have to admit the idea that an animal had mauled Julia—I glanced at Caleb and thought, hmm, maybe even a shifter—made my stomach turn. I'd seen death before. Hel-*lo*, vampire here. But looking at Julia's mangled body, I admit her death struck me as undignified and wrong.

"Gretta?"

We heard Lilly's voice behind us. We turned and saw her standing at the corner of the house. "Magistrate Williamson will be here soon," she said. "He said to leave the body alone and to keep everyone in the parlor."

With the cavalry on the way, there wasn't much for us to do other than go into the house and wait. I wasn't sure how paranormal murder was handled in the outside world. In Broken Heart, we had a security force that kept the order and protected its citizens. I wondered what this magistrate would do once he got here.

My question was answered less than an hour later when he arrived. With his trench coat, gray fedora, and designer leather shoes, he looked like he'd fallen out of the movie *Casablanca*. He removed the trench coat and hat, which he handed to Gretta, and revealed his tailored gray pin-stripped suit. He wore his wavy brown hair short, but it had enough length to it to require a good haircut and style knowledge. He had a square jaw with a dimpled chin, angled cheeks, thick eyebrows, and a sharp gaze.

"Good evening, everyone," he said as he entered the parlor. He had a British accent. I felt a chill come over me as I realized this situation had gone way past *Murder, She Wrote* and right into *Law & Order*.

Dun-dun.

"My name is Magistrate Andrew Williamson. I will need to talk to each of you separately. For the moment, I must ask everyone to stay in the parlor until I've finished conducting the interviews."

"Is it just you?" Duane asked, suspicion in his voice. "Where are the rest of the people?"

Magistrate Williamson turned his gaze onto the true crime writer. "What people?"

"You know, detectives and people in Tyvek suits taking pictures and dusting for fingerprints," answered Margaret, her Maine accent adding extra syllables to her words. She pointed to Duane who was leaning against the hearth, pretending like he was some kind of expert. "Don't you think, Mr. Cutter?" She turned her gaze to Magistrate Williamson, looking almost like a proud mama. "He's a true crime writer," she said. "Mr. Cutter knows all about this stuff."

The magistrate didn't seem impressed by Duane's writer credentials. And, in fact, Duane looked embarrassed by Margaret's depiction of him. But he still looked at the magistrate with doubts in his eyes. "I've never heard of a magistrate conducting a murder investigation."

The magistrate's brows rose. "Why do you think she was murdered?"

Duane reared back, surprised. "Because she—" His eyes darted toward Serena. "The way she looked. She didn't do that to herself."

"Cause of death has not been determined," said Magistrate Williamson. "Unless you are aware of the manner of Mrs. Davenport's death?"

"It's Miss Davenport," said Duane. "I know nothing about how she died."

"Ah." The magistrate looked around. "As I stated, I'll be doing the interviews."

"What will happen to my mother?" asked Serena.

"We're taking care of her," he said gently. "We'll take you to her later, Miss Davenport. I am quite sorry for your loss."

Serena nodded, her mouth trembling as her eyes filled with tears again. Then collapsed into Evan's arms and cried more. Poor kid.

The magistrate moved deeper into the parlor. "We'll have a chat in the kitchen where there's privacy and, I'm told, warm cinnamon rolls and freshly made tea." His gaze swept over us. "I'd like to start with the young lady who discovered Miss Davenport."

Hannah rose from the couch. "That would be me." She looked at her husband who sat next to her, holding her hand. "Can Caleb come with me?"

"I'm afraid not."

Hannah looked like she'd rather throw herself into the fireplace than go into the kitchen alone with Magistrate Williamson. Reluctantly she rounded the couch and headed toward the parlor's exit. The magistrate stood at the doorway and gestured for her to go ahead of him.

Hannah returned to the parlor, her expression pensive, and then it was Caleb's turn. Caleb didn't look too worse for wear when he came back. The magistrate called in Duane. After Duane finished giving his statement, it was Evan and Serena's turn.

I wasn't sure why the magistrate allowed Evan and Serena to be interviewed together when he wouldn't allow Hannah to take Caleb with her. Maybe because it was Serena's mother who died—not to mention that the girl was due to give birth today. He probably felt like she might need extra support.

The magistrate called Claire next—and the he talked to her for quite a while. Then it was Margaret's turn, but her interview seemed to go the quickest. I wondered if that was because she was a human or because she had nothing important to add. She'd been in her room when the drama with Julia unfolded. And she'd been in the parlor crocheting when Julia's body was found.

"Mrs. O'Halloran?"

I looked over my shoulder at the detective. He stood to the side of the parlor doorway. Patrick squeezed my hand before I stood up and followed Magistrate Williamson through the dining room and into the kitchen.

Or maybe it was more like the lion's den.

CHAPTER ELEVEN

Unlike the rest of the bed-and-breakfast with its Golden Girls theme, the kitchen was surprisingly modern with granite counters, stainless steel appliances and Travertine floor tile. I suspected Lilly designed the modern space. She struck me as a tidy person and everything about the kitchen had an everything-in-its-place feel.

I sat on a stool at the kitchen island with its butcher-block top. As promised, warm cinnamon rolls on a large platter and a tea service with multiple cups sat on the island. Those cinnamon rolls smelled so, so good.

"I know you're a vampire," he said.

"You do?"

He pulled out a wallet and flipped it open, showing me a shiny silver badge in the shape of a pentagram. Magistrate Inspector Andrew Williamson was engraved on the metal along with a badge number and a symbol I didn't recognize. He flipped the wallet the other way and another badge appeared, this one was more familiar. It was gold and had Magistrate Andrew Williamson etched on it along with a different badge number. "This one is for the humans," he said.

"It's enchanted to give me the authority I need to investigate when humans are involved."

"You're not a vampire," I said. I looked him over. "Or a shifter."

"Necromancer," he said. "Makes the job a lot easier."

"Holy crap. Did you necromance-whatever Julia and find out what happened?"

He lifted his eyebrows. "Not that easy, I'm afraid. I understand that you and your husband came to the bed-and-breakfast for a vacation?"

"Yes."

"When did you arrive?"

I bet a two-pound box of Godiva chocolate truffles that he already knew the answer to the question. Magistrate Williamson struck me as a very organized, prepared, and intelligent individual. "About midnight," I said. "It was raining so hard I thought Noah's Ark was gonna show up."

Amusement flashed in his gaze. "So, you met Miss Davenport for the first time last night?"

"Magistrate Williamson, patience is not my strong suit," I said. "I'll tell you everything from start to finish. Yes, I met Julia Davenport last night for the first time. She was a total bitch. She treated everyone, including her own daughter, like dog crap. When Evan arrived, she tried to kill him with her magic. If my husband hadn't stepped in front of him that kid would've been toast."

"That infuriated you."

"Yeah, it did."

"You pulled out swords?"

I figured he got that information from one of the people in the room when all the drama happened. I stood up and made my short swords appear.

"The Ruadan swords." He looked at the blades with

amazement. "I've heard of them—but I've never seen them with my own eyes. May I?"

"Knock yourself out." I put the swords on the countertop. Detective Williamson picked them up one at a time by the jeweled hilts and examined the blades. I realized his interest in my swords went beyond their historical and magical value. He was looking for evidence I had used my blades to murder Julia.

"No blood," I said. "I didn't stab Julia to death."

"You had plenty of time to clean them." Magistrate Williamson glanced at me. "You threatened her."

"I did. She tried to kill the boyfriend who wants to take care of Serena and their baby. Then she used her magic on my husband. And then that crazy woman threw her killer magic at me."

He put down the swords on the butcher-block. "You're not making yourself out to be innocent, Mrs. O'Halloran."

"I'm not guilty. And call me Jessica." I picked up my swords.

"I'd like to take those into evidence, Jessica," said the magistrate. "We have a paranormal version of CSI. They'll need to examine the blades."

"Yeah, that's not gonna happen." I disappeared my swords.

He blinked. "You understand that I represent the supernatural authorities, do you not?"

"Sure. But I'm still not giving you the swords bestowed by Brigid, the goddess who forged them."

"Ah. I'd heard as much. You know the Celtic goddess of healing?"

"Related by marriage," I said. "She is Patrick's grandmother."

He was silent for a moment. "Are you trying to thwart my investigation, Jessica?"

"Not at all. I'll cooperate with you—except for handing over the swords that Ruadan himself used to fight the Fomorians." I looked him straight in the eye. "I didn't kill Julia Davenport."

He tried to stare a hole through me. "You could have."

"But I didn't. Aside from not liking her very much and using my weapons for self-defense, husband-defense, and human-defense, I had no reason to kill her."

The magistrate studied me a moment more. His expression softened. "You're a mother, aren't you, Jessica?"

"What gave it away?" I asked, somewhat sarcastically.

"The way others have described you. I see what they mean. So, are you? A mother?"

"Yes. Three kids. All grown. The youngest started college a few weeks ago."

He nodded. "You probably look at Serena and see how lost she is. How much pain she's in."

"Although I'm a bloodsucker, I have a heart."

"I wouldn't blame you for trying to help her."

Wait... he thought I stabbed Julia to death because I empathized with her daughter? I glared at him. "Are you saying my sympathy for Serena drove me to kill her mother?"

"You got overwhelmed, right? You're a mother with three healthy, grown children. And here's a beautiful girl with an awful parent. You see everything happening to her. It makes you angry." His voice was soft with empathy and his eyes gleamed with understanding. "Perhaps you confronted Julia and let your fury override your common decency. Is that what happened?"

"What is wrong with you?" I asked, appalled by his accusation. "You don't go around murdering people because they're mean. Sure I wish Serena had a better lot in life. And I will help her however I can. But murdering her mother? No. Hell, no."

I wouldn't look away from his gaze, now hard with accusation. Finally, he relented. Then he nodded. "I believe you."

"Just like that?"

"I have good instincts, Jessica. And I'd bet my hat, you do, too."

"Your *hat*?"

His lips curved into a half-smile. "You don't understand how much I love my fedora. I'd loathe losing it in a bet."

"I feel the same way about chocolate," I said. I wasn't thrilled about being accused of murder, but I also understood that the magistrate was doing his job. Other than that, I liked Andrew Williamson. "Any more questions, Magistrate?"

"Call me Andrew," he invited. "The interview is concluded for now."

"Great." I got up and headed toward the exit.

"You're very unusual, Jessica."

"I've been called worse," I said, still heading toward the door.

"You misunderstand. I mean unusual in an interesting way. You didn't do the one thing everyone who's walked into this kitchen has done."

I stopped and half-turned to look at him. "Yeah? What's that?"

"You didn't lie."

◆ ◆ ◆

After Magistrate Williamson interviewed my husband, Patrick rejoined me on the couch.

"Did he accuse you of lying?" I asked.

Patrick's dark brows rose. "No. Did he accuse you?"

"Nope. He said I was the only who didn't lie. But he hadn't interviewed you yet, so... did you tell a fib?"

"And what fib would that be, Mrs. Fletcher?"

"Har-de-har."

Patrick's gaze met mine. "I didn't tell any fibs because there weren't any to tell. We didn't kill that vile woman."

"But someone here did," I whispered. "Would why everyone else lie to the magistrate?"

"Some people have secrets, *mo chroí*. They might do anything to protect them."

I absorbed that comment and then turned it over in my mind. Could these people have secrets they wanted to protect? And what would they have to do with Julia anyways? Serena and Evan had a motive—but not an opportunity, right? At least not with Claire guarding them. Julia insulted Duane and his novels but that wasn't a reason to hack her to death. I mean, he didn't even know about the paranormal shenanigans going on. Serena wondered last night if Duane knew her mother. Did his lie to the magistrate have something to do with the fact he had knowledge about the supernatural world? Or had only he lied about knowing the victim prior to meeting her at the bed-and-breakfast?

Why would he—heck, why would anyone—kill Julia so viciously?

Like the way an ax murderer might hack someone to death, for instance.

Would Duane take his research that far?

No way. He struck me as arrogant, but not as insane.

My gaze landed on Margaret, who'd gone back to crocheting the longest scarf ever. What would she have to lie about? I couldn't believe this little old lady had some kind of nefarious purpose.

Now, Claire—she seemed like a woman with secrets. Her own. Or someone else's. She had to uphold doctor-patient confidentiality, right? Claire probably knew a thing or two about Julia and Serena and she didn't like Julia at all. But I couldn't see her chasing the witch down and slashing her to death. Not when she could create a poison or a curse or whatever and take her out. No fuss. No muss.

I glanced at the newlyweds. They had no motive to do away with the witch. They had an opportunity, sure. And they had means, especially in their wolf forms. But no reason to end Julia's life. Except for a thrill kill. As freaked out as Hannah got about the Willescane murders, I couldn't imagine her gleefully shredding a person. Not if she couldn't handle ghosts haunting the bed-and-breakfast.

I looked behind me and observed Gretta and Lilly by the serving table having a hushed conversation. Whatever they were talking about, it was intense. Gretta grabbed Lilly's arms, and Lilly responded by wrenching herself out of her sister's grasp.

"I'm fine," said Lilly through gritted teeth. "Stop fussing."

"We should've never allowed Serena and her mother to come here," said Gretta, her voice worried. "It's set you off again, hasn't it? It's been decades, Lil. Can't you let it go?"

"When you bring a baby girl into this world and then have her ripped from your arms by your own family—you can talk to me about letting go. I mourn her every day, Gretta." She pressed a fist against her heart. "Every. Single. Day."

"Lilly—"

Lilly shook her head and turned her back on her sister. She busied herself with stacking mugs on the serving table. Gretta's expression was pure misery. She left her sister alone and crossed the room to stoke the fire.

Lilly was still mourning the child she'd never gotten to raise. Her family had taken away her daughter—the same as Julia intended to take away Serena's baby girl. It had to be torture for Lilly to watch Julia treat Serena so poorly and know the girl's fate was so much like her own had been.

The magistrate had said everyone who'd stepped into the kitchen had lied.

And that meant the twins, too, right?

What did they have to hide? Why would they lie? And about what?

Would Lilly, who was as sympathetic as I was to Serena's plight, do what Magistrate Williamson had accused me of doing? Murder Julia to protect the teenager and her unborn child?

The magistrate strode into the parlor. "No one is to leave the bed-and-breakfast until—" He glanced at Serena. "Um, until the... situation has been resolved."

"You mean until someone admits to killing my mother," said Serena dully. She looked pale, her eyes swollen from crying. She gripped Evan as though if she didn't have someone to hold on to, she might disappear. "What about her?" Serena nodded toward me. "She had swords pointed right at Mom. She could've killed her!"

CHAPTER TWELVE

"Swords?" Duane stared at me from the chair he occupied. "You have *swords*?"

Oh, crap. I looked at Magistrate Williamson, thinking he needed to fix this paranormal collision of facts in front of the human, but it was Margaret who came to my rescue.

"Swords? My goodness." Margaret tittered. "I only have crochet hooks." She lifted her yarn project as if to show us her "weaponry."

"But Serena—"

"Is tired," stated Evan. "She needs to lie down."

Serena looked exhausted, and she allowed Evan to help her to her feet. She walked past the couch and paused next to where I sat. "I'm s-sorry. You protected Evan. I shouldn't have a-accused you."

"Oh, honey," I said, reaching out to squeeze her hand, "you don't owe me an apology. Don't you worry. Evan here will take care of you. You'll get through this."

She nodded, appearing more miserable than ever, and then she and Evan left the parlor. The stairs creaked as the human helped his girlfriend navigate the steps.

I turned back and saw Duane's gaze fixated on me. Well, great. Margaret's attempt to direct attention away from me hadn't worked. But with Magistrate Williamson still in the room, I don't think Duane had the balls to pursue it further.

I think we should glamour him, I sent to Patrick.

I don't know if the magistrate would appreciate us wiping Duane's memory of anything right now.

Well, he better not give me any shit.

Perish the thought, mo chroí. I think you scare him.

Ha, ha.

"So, we can't leave?" asked Hannah. She'd opted to sit on the floor near the hearth. Caleb sat behind her rubbing her shoulders. "We answered your questions. You can't make us stay here."

"Would you rather I arrest you and hold you as a person of interest?"

"You can't arrest her without cause." Mr. True Crime was running his mouth again. Now, he thought he was a lawyer.

"I can arrest her for obstruction of justice," said the magistrate.

Duane pressed his lips together and butted out.

"Would you really do that?" asked Margaret. "That seems rather harsh."

But it wasn't. The rules for parakind differed from those for humans. You had to take a hard line with creatures with supernatural abilities. And Hannah knew it. Her face fell as she realized she would have to stay in the bed-and-breakfast.

Neither Caleb nor Hannah seemed to have an obvious motive. And what happened to Julia was no accident. Someone—something—had mauled, or chopped, her to death. That struck me as personal. You'd have to be furious or crazy to tear at someone's flesh until they died.

"I'll say good night." Magistrate Williamson nodded to

everyone and then he said, "Mrs. O'Halloran, do you have a moment?"

"Sure." I followed him out of the parlor and into the foyer. Gretta handed him his coat and fedora and then excused herself.

"Are there really CSI and other detectives out there with Julia's body?" I asked. "Because I don't think there are."

"Why?"

I shrugged. "Like you said, I have instincts."

"Ah. Well, I never said there were, did I? I'm a one-man show tonight," he said. "I told you I was a necromancer. I used spellwork to copy the crime scene, which I will then recreate in my lab. My magic transported Mrs. Davenport's body to my team's facility, where she will be both magically and physically autopsied."

"Your team?"

"Yes."

"Like the supernatural A-Team? Let me guess. You're The Face."

He grinned. "You think I'm good-looking, don't you?"

"Have you seen my husband?" I retorted. "He's good-looking. But you're okay, I guess."

His grin widened. "Thanks. To assuage your curiosity, I'm Hannibal."

"I can't wait to meet your Mr. T."

"Oh, I think you can."

I rolled my eyes. "What don't you tell me what you need?"

"I would like you to keep an eye on things," he said. He reached into the trench coat's side pocket and handed me a business card. "Should anything happen before I return, you can call me at that number."

The plain white card had Magistrate Andrew Williamson

and a phone number printed on it in black ink. I squinted. "What's the stuff under the number?"

"A spell that transports me to wherever you are. However, I'd appreciate you saving that for an emergency."

"Huh. How very Harry Potter of you."

He laughed. "If only Floo powder were really a thing," he said. "That would be marvelous."

"You don't need Floo powder, though, do you? You can translocate."

"Yes, but not in the same way as vampires."

"Or witches?"

He looked at me, his brow furrowed. "Witches?"

"Can't they magic themselves to places the way vampires —or necromancers—do?" Because that was what Lilly had suggested about Julia's disappearance.

"It's possible," he said. "But it would take a lot of power and spellwork to do it. Vampires have fae magic—that's more powerful than the tricks witches learn. Witches have to draw power from somewhere, or someone, else then learn to manipulate it. As you know fae magic is natural sorcery, imbued in your blood, and much easier to use."

"If you say so." I tucked the card into my back jean pocket. "Lilly said Julia could translocate. I thought Julia might've magicked herself off the island after we discovered she wasn't in her cottage."

"Hmm. If she could do that," he mused, "why didn't she translocate away from the murderer?"

"Good question." What if Julia couldn't transport herself anywhere? If so, why would Lilly even say something like that? Unless she knew why Julia was missing. Whoa. Had Lilly killed the witch? I figured she didn't like Julia any better than the rest of us, but if she had torn apart Julia, why would she leave the body on the side of the house for anyone to find?

The magistrate's expression turned brooding. "Julia Davenport was a powerful witch with more than her share of enemies." His gaze met mine. "Someone on this island killed her."

"Who do you suspect?"

"Ah. Nice try, Jessica, but my theories must remain my own. Most detective work is done with online research, phone calls, and victimology. I'll work as fast as I can because we need to find the murderer before anyone leaves this island."

"Well, hurry. I don't want to be stuck here with someone who has an ax fetish."

He chuckled. "I like you, Jessica."

"Why wouldn't you? I'm awesome." I patted my back pocket. "You want to deputize me or something?" I was only half-joking. Look at me now, Jessica Fletcher. Wouldn't you be proud?

"I'm afraid not. I'm not telling you to do anything." He adjusted his hat. "You might get people to talk to you. If they say anything of import... let me know."

"Yeah. Okay. And while I'm solving your case what will you be doing?"

"Drinking pots of tea and awaiting my call?" she said.

"Your sarcasm sounds very pretty with that accent."

A genuine smile crossed his mouth. "Until we meet again, Jessica."

After Magistrate Williamson left out the front door undoubtedly so he could poof back to wherever without being in sight of the humans. I returned to the parlor and sat next to Patrick. He put his arm around my shoulders. "What did the magistrate want?"

"To arrest me for murder, but then he felt sorry for me and I said he'd let me get away with it this time."

Patrick lifted one dark eyebrow. "Did he now?"

"No. He wants me to be his snoop."

Patrick stared at me for so long I got itchy. "What?" I asked testily.

"Do you find that a strange request?"

"I find everything about our getaway strange. I threatened a mean witch who was murdered. There's a teenaged girl who's gonna pop out a baby at any second. Her human boyfriend stole a ferry to get here—so who knows what else he's capable of. Let's not forget the nosy writer who thinks he's an expert on everything or the crocheting grandmother. We have vampire twins who know more about this house's history than they're telling. Werewolf newlyweds who are the only creatures around here with claws sharp enough to rip open Julia." I shook my head. "Not to mention the root doctor."

"Didn't you want more excitement in your life?"

I snorted a laugh. "Careful what you wish for, is that what you're telling me?"

Patrick kissed my forehead. "One thing we have never had, darlin', is a boring life together."

"Ain't that the truth."

I looked around the room. Margaret was crocheting away. Duane was typing furiously. Neither Lilly nor Gretta were about, but they were probably off doing proprietor-type stuff. We were also missing a certain werewolf couple.

"What happened to Caleb and Hannah?" I asked.

"Went to bed," said Patrick. "At least that's what they said. Hannah seems the jittery sort."

"I don't understand her reaction to Duane's tale of horror," I said. "It's not like the ax murderer will suddenly come back and hack everyone to death again."

Patrick frowned. "You mean like chopping up a witch?"

"You think those marks on Julia's body were made from an ax?"

"I don't know what made those injuries. It could've been claws, but did you see any bite marks? An animal attack would've left damage from claws and teeth. Animals—even shifters—go for the neck. And her face was barely touched."

My hubby had a point. "Yeah, well, I can't believe an ax murderer from 1926 popped by for a visit."

"It seems the least likely scenario."

But not something we could cross off the list, either. This was a bed- and-breakfast run by vampires and lots of parakind vacationed here. If the killer of the Willescane family was supernatural he—or she—could still be around. Maybe he even returned here for a celebratory-anniversary killing spree. It was a stretch, but yikes. I got how Hannah felt about being in the house. Ghosts didn't scare me. An ax-wielding monster sure did.

Gretta bustled in from the kitchen holding a teapot. "Does anyone want tea? Given all the stress of what's happened, I made a nice calming chamomile."

"I'll take a cup, dear," said Margaret. "Two sugars, please."

Everyone else declined tea, so Gretta made Margaret's cup and then set about straightening the parlor.

I missed taking care of hearth and home.

Sure, I complained about the kids leaving their messes everywhere, but there was something lonely about walking through a clean house. No jackets tossed onto the kitchen counter while the offender rummaged in the fridge for a snack. No glitter smeared across the dining room table from a crafting frenzy. No zombie parts left in the living room to elicit shrieks of horror. Okay. I didn't really miss the zombie parts. But the other stuff? Definitely.

A bed-and-breakfast was always hearth and home—and there was always someone to feed, to tuck in, to converse with, and to hug. Affection. Warmth. Companionship.

Now that I thought about it, I understood the Thompson

Twins desire to own and operate a bed-and-breakfast. Maybe running a B&B seemed an odd way to spend your eternity. Maybe they'd done everything else and this was just how they wanted to spend their next fifty years. But you know what?

I think I would like it, too.

CHAPTER THIRTEEN

"I think I'll take my tea to the cottage and read before bedtime." Margaret stuffed her crochet and yarn into her little tote, put it on her arm, and picked up her teacup. She smiled. "Night, all."

"I'll walk with you," I said.

"I'm sure I'll be fine, dear."

"Neither one of you should be outside in the dark with a killer on the loose," said Duane. He looked at Patrick. "Are you going to let your wife and a senior citizen go out there alone?"

I opened my mouth to tell Duane where he could shove his misogyny, but Patrick answered before I could.

"Yes," he said. "Jessica doesn't need my permission—or my protection."

Duane's lip pressed together. He shot my husband a dark look before returning his attention to the MacBook.

I looked at Patrick. "Be right back."

My husband nodded in acknowledgement. Then he winked at me.

God, I loved that man.

Others murmured their goodnights, too. Margaret shuffled across the parlor, the ears of her bunny slippers flip-flopping against the floor.

I felt sorry for Margaret. She seemed apart from the rest of us, not just because she was a human, but also because she hadn't shared anything about herself. She seemed busy enough with her crochet project and friendly enough to everyone she spoke with. But still. I wondered about her family—about her knowledge of parakind. Everyone had a story. What was hers?

I followed Margaret to the back porch. Once we got outside, she turned and took the stone path. We walked together, but the wind was relentless and made it difficult to talk. We crossed a section of lawn and stepped onto the porch of the white cottage with its pitched roof and black shutters. Surrounded by rose bushes, it looked like a house right out of a fairy tale.

"This is nice," I said.

"What?"

"I said it's nice." I spoke louder, but Margaret shook her head.

"I can't hear you, dear. The wind is a monster tonight." She waved at me. "Come inside."

She opened the door, and I followed her into a living room with its own fireplace. The area was too small for full-sized furniture, but looked comfy enough with the recliner and loveseat arranged in front of the hearth. There was just enough room for the coffee table, which was covered with yarn and crochet books. The overhead light cast an eerie yellow glow over the otherwise cozy room.

"I need to put my things away, Jessica. Have a seat." She put her teacup onto the coffee table and paused. "You're a vampire, too, right?"

"Yes," I said.

"So tea or coffee is out of the question. I'm sorry I don't have any... er, blood."

"I'm good, Mrs. Maple," I said. "Thank you."

"Call me Margaret, dear." She disappeared into a door on the right side of the living room. Behind the love seat was the entrance to the kitchen. I pushed through the swinging doors for a quick peek. On the left was the galley kitchen that might fit two people if they didn't mind brushing elbows. On the right, a square table with two chairs.

I plopped onto the love seat in the living room. A moment later, Margaret joined me. She picked up her teacup and sat in the recliner.

"Would you like me to start a fire for you?" I asked.

"No, thank you. I'm off to bed soon."

I figured that was a hint, but I decided I couldn't leave without asking a question or two.

"Margaret, how did you learn about parakind?"

She smiled. "My parents. They were human, but they knew about the supernatural. I was raised knowing all about vampires." Her smile flickered. "I'm not scared by the things that go bump in the night."

"Sounds like you're perfect for the job here," I said.

"Ayuh." She laughed. "If I say so myself. Lived in Maine all my life, but I just moved to Bar Harbor. Glad to get the job. Good thing I like it out here in the willie-wacks."

I interpreted "willie-wacks" as the Okie equivalent of the back of beyond AKA middle of nowhere. "You have kids, Margaret?"

"No. My husband and I chose careers over family." She looked at me over the rim of her teacup. "Does that surprise you?"

"A little," I admitted. "You seem like a... well, like a grandmother."

"Do I now?" She shook her head. "I don't regret the

choice. Neither did my Harold. We had a good life, the two us." She sighed. "Harold died of cancer a few years back. Still miss him."

"I'm so sorry," I said.

"Thank you," she said. "You are the finest kind." She leaned forward, her eyes filled with concern. "Jessica, do you ever regret becoming a vampire?"

"No," I said. "Not that I had a choice. I got killed and woke up undead. My kids were fourteen and nine and their dad had passed away the year before. So, no. I don't regret it."

She nodded. "I understand. And your husband? Is he the one who saved you?"

"In more ways than one," I said. "How much do you know about vampires?"

"Hmm. Ruadan—he was the first vampire. Thousands of years ago. He Turned six others, making them master vampires. So there are seven bloodlines, right?"

"Actually, there are eight."

"Oh. Do tell."

"We have eight vampire Families and each bloodline has different powers. For example, I'm part of the Family Ruadan, thus *Sidhe* magic is in my blood. Besides the general vampire abilities of speed, strength, and glamour, I can fly."

"Like a bird?"

"Not exactly. I can rise into the air, hover like a helicopter, or take off across the sky like a jet. Well, when it's not pouring buckets," I said. "Not even vampires want to fly in the rain."

"Don't blame you." She looked into her teacup before taking a sip. "Is your husband Family Ruadan, too?"

"Yes," I said. I didn't want to freak her out by admitting Patrick was literally Ruadan's family.

"How does vampire marriage work?" she asked. "It's for a hundred years, right?"

"Yes. It's called the Binding."

The original eight vampires put together a powerful, unbreakable spell called the Binding. The Binding prevents vampires from using their preternatural gifts to seduce unwilling humans. Vampires controlled their baser urges when the consequences were steep.

If you hook up with a mortal, that's your bed partner for a century. If they die? Yeah, you're still hitched to them. Magically. As in, you can't be too far away from your mate or you'll die, too. If your partner dies before the hundred years is over, then you carry around their corpse, bones, or ashes with you. If you think the solution was to Turn the human into a vampire, well, not all humans make the transition.

The rest die horrible deaths.

I wasn't conscious during the whole Make-Jess-a-Vampire process, so I don't remember anything. But I have witnessed vampire-making, and it's not pretty.

"I can't imagine living forever. I'm in my twilight years," she mused. "Nearly at the end of my journey. I hope you don't take offense, dear, but we're not meant to live eternally. At least not on this earth. It's against the natural order." She put down her teacup, her gaze on mine. "Everything dies except for vampires."

"We can die," I said.

"I'm not talking about walking out into the sun or getting your head lopped off," said Margaret. "You are capable of living forever. Don't you find that odd?"

"Everything about being a vampire is odd, but you get used to it."

"Well, as you said. You didn't have a choice. And your children? How are they?"

"All grown up," I said. "We just sent my youngest to college. Patrick and I adopted a two-year-old boy, Rich, after we got together. Now, he's a freshman at Oklahoma University."

"How nice." Margaret yawned, stretching her arms over her head. Her movements were exaggerated, designed to make me realize I'd overstayed my welcome. "Oh, my goodness. I think it's time for me to go to bed."

This time, I wouldn't ignore Margaret's not-so-subtle hint. I stood up. "Thanks for the nice chat."

"You, too, Jessica."

I bid her good night and left. The wind welcomed me with sharp, cold gusts. I wrapped my arms around myself, closed my eyes, and thought about the back porch. In a matter of seconds, I'd zapped myself there. I hurried into the warmth of the house and returned to the parlor. I slid next to Patrick who was scrolling through his Kindle. He smiled at me. "Did you tuck her in, love?"

"No," I said. "But I would have if she'd let me."

He chuckled. Then he leaned down and kissed the top of my head.

I watched Gretta flit around the room straightening knick-knacks and returning board games to the shelves next to the hearth.

"Why don't you take a load off?" I asked.

"I'll rest when I'm dead," she said with her tinkling laugh. "I love puttering around and taking care of the house and our guests. You probably think that's not an ideal way for a—" Her gaze flicked to Duane. "Well, for a girl to spend her time."

"I think it's wonderful," I said. "We're lucky. We have all the time in the world to figure out what makes us happy." I grabbed my husband's hand. "And I'm super lucky because I already know what that is."

Patrick smiled and then guided my hand to his mouth where he brushed his lips across my knuckles. The look of love in his gaze warmed me to my toes. "I love you, mo chroí."

"I love you back."

"You two are adorable," said Gretta. Her smile was genuine though her gaze seemed distant—as if she'd gotten lost in a memory. She shook her head. "I am sorry about all the trouble. I swear our bed-and-breakfast is usually peaceful and relaxing."

"I believe you," I said. "I love everything about this place."

"Thank you. Well, there is a pile of dishes with my name on it," said Gretta. She picked up a stack of magazines. "Do you need anything?"

I shook my head.

"Duane," she said. "How about you? Need anything?"

"I'm good. Thanks."

She nodded and then left the parlor.

I turned my attention to Duane. "How's the book coming along?"

"Fine," he said. He hesitated, looking down at his computer, and then back up at us. "I know why the Willescanes came to the island."

"Oh, really?"

He looked eager to share his information. You gotta love know-it-alls. They rarely kept anything to themselves. He said, "Bootlegging."

"You said that before," I pointed out. "You thought maybe the Vinettas put him out here to smuggle in Canadian booze."

"I've conducted further research online and I think I can prove that's the case. Willescane owned the island. He built the house. I'm sure there's a hidden room somewhere in this house where they kept the alcohol."

"Why have a secret room?" I asked. "You think the police would bother raiding this house?"

"Willescane was paranoid. He took all precautions." He looked pleased with himself. "It's a perfect set-up. Even Al Capone used to smuggle alcohol from Canada. A lot of rum runners were from Nova Scotia." He pointed, presumably toward Nova Scotia. I wasn't great with geography. "I suspect there's a tunnel that leads to the dock, too." He snapped his laptop shut. "Store the booze in the secret room and at night, cart it to the boats. Short trip down the coast, right to the Vinettas' warehouses." He nodded. "I bet that's how the older daughters got away from the ax murderer. Ran down the tunnel to the dock, got on a boat, and took off."

"Do you think competing smugglers might've taken out the Willescanes?" asked my husband.

Duane frowned. "Not at all. I think it's the same killer I've been tracking through the U.S."

"Have you made any connections between the Willescane deaths and the Axeman of New Orleans?" I asked.

His frown deepened. "I can't share that information."

Translation: *I have no evidence for my theory and I will not admit it.*

"I think I'll turn in," said Duane, probably to forestall more questions from us. He stood up, holding his MacBook and lap desk. "Good night."

We said our goodnights and then Patrick and I were alone in the parlor. I snuggled against my hubby and stared at the fire while he scrolled through the news on his Kindle. I hadn't seen Claire, but I assumed she was in the room with the kids. I hoped that Serena wouldn't go into labor until after the weekend. I'd never had a home birth before, so I didn't know a lot about it. Still. Giving birth, especially for the first time, was scary enough without the extra stress of doing it in a strange place in the middle of nowhere and with a murderer on the loose.

Gretta returned and placed clean mugs on the back serving table. She'd barely put down the cups before Lilly rushed into the parlor holding a stack of towels. Her eyes were as wide as saucers. "Caleb and Hannah are gone!"

CHAPTER FOURTEEN

"What?" Gretta stopped stacking coffee mugs and stared at her sister. "Maybe Caleb and Hannah went for a run."

"They took their suitcases."

"To go where?" I asked. "There's no way off the island."

"Sweet lord. You don't think they'd attempt to take the ferry, do you?" Gretta placed a hand against her chest. "Surely, they wouldn't do something so dangerous."

"Well, they can't go anywhere," I said. "The ferry's broken, right?"

"They don't know that," she said.

"But they know the ferry's at the dock," pointed out Patrick. "They must've overheard us talking about it."

"They might think they can fix it," I said.

Why had the werewolves bailed? Had I been wrong about those two? Did they murder Julia? She and Caleb found the body. What if they found Julia and killed her and then came to get us?

The idea rang hollow.

"Let's check the parking lot," said Patrick. "Do you know which car they drove?"

"Yes," said Lilly. "It's a Ford hatchback. Red."

Patrick and I headed outside. When we got the parking lot, we studied the six cars—our sedan, a silver Jaguar, a white Lincoln Continental, the Mazda Miata, a battered light blue truck and a white minivan with Thompson Twins Bed & Breakfast painted on the side. Gretta was right about the wind. It whipped around us, turning my hair into tiny stingers as the strands struck my face and neck.

"I bet the Jaguar is Julia's. And the Lincoln must belong to Margaret."

"Why?"

"Because it screams little old lady from Bar Harbor."

"Uh-huh. And the Miata?"

"True Crime Duane."

"We know the truck belongs to Evan—he said as much last night." Patrick studied the rest of the parking. "There's no red hatchback."

"And there doesn't appear to be a car for Claire."

"Maybe she didn't bring one or maybe the Miata is hers." He pointed to the minivan. "At least one person must've arrived on the ferry and gotten picked up from the pier."

"That makes sense." I put my hands on my hips. "Magistrate Williamson made it clear he had no problem arresting them. Where do they think they're going? It will be worse for them once the paranormal police catch up. Running away makes them look guilty. Do you think we should call the magistrate?"

"Not yet," said Patrick. "They're missing. We don't know that they're dead."

"Well, I don't think they're the killers, either."

"Maybe they are," said Patrick. "Otherwise, why would they try to leave now?"

I had no answer. A few seconds later, Gretta and Lilly joined us outside.

"They took their car," I said.

"We have go to the dock," said Gretta.

"We'll go," said Patrick. He looked at me. "We'll drive the car. It'll take longer than zapping ourselves there, but we may need to drive Caleb and Hannah back with us."

He meant we'd make them get in the car and return to the B&B because we would not let them take their stupid selves back to the mainland on a broken down ferry.

"What's going on?"

I looked over my shoulder and saw Claire. She wore an oversized sweatshirt, jeans, and hiking boots. She'd put her hair into a clip, but the fierce wind loosed strands from the binding.

"Caleb and Hannah have done a runner," I said. "Patrick and I will try to find them."

"What the hell are they thinking?" asked Claire.

Above us, the storm clouds thickened and swirled. Lightning flashed and then thunder cracked.

"We better hurry," I said. "We need to get back before that storm breaks."

"Let's go," said Patrick.

We hurried to the car, and Patrick wasted no time starting the engine and backing out of the parking space. There weren't any street lamps on the narrow road, and our headlights barely penetrated into the deep night. Good thing we had vampire vision, or the wild drive to the pier would be a lot more harrowing.

When we got to the dock, it was clear something was wrong. I saw the red Ford hatchback parked at the end of the road. Both the doors were wide open. The lights were on inside the car, too.

"*Damnu air*," muttered Patrick. "This can't be good."

He pulled up to the abandoned car, and we got out. Closer to the ocean, the wind was a hundred times worse—and had a salty bite. Also, it smelled like dead fish and rotting seaweed. Ew.

Patrick went to the driver's side, and I went to the passenger's. We looked inside and studied the interior. Their suitcases had been tossed into the back seat. Hannah's purse was still on the floor. The car had been turned off, but the keys hadn't been taken.

"Where did they go?" I asked.

Patrick shook his head. "No blood. No anything. It looks like they left in a hurry, though."

"Let's check the dock. Maybe they tried to take the ferry without putting their car on it."

Patrick and I used our vampire speed to zip down the dock to where the ferry was tied up. It slished and sloshed in the swirling, black water. No lights. No running engine. Worse, no Caleb or Hannah. Patrick and I climbed aboard and found every door and latch locked tight.

"Where did they go?" I yelled over the whipping wind.

"Maybe they got spooked and walked back to the bed-and-breakfast."

"Wouldn't they take the road? We didn't see them on the way here."

"They probably shifted and went through the woods."

I could only hope my husband was right. We returned to the newlyweds' car. Patrick took the keys, and we shut the doors. Then Patrick locked the vehicle.

"Wait. What if they come back? They won't be able to get in and they won't know we have their keys."

"You think I should leave their keys in the car?" Patrick looked at me like I was crazy.

"Who will steal it?" I asked. "We're on a freaking island in the middle of the ocean."

"I'll leave it unlocked, but I'm taking the keys. We can't risk them trying to get it onto the ferry."

"We could take their car back with us," I said. Thunder rumbled and I looked up at the roiling clouds. The threatening storm would unleash its fury any time now. "Never mind. If they come back here, they might need the car as shelter to wait out the storm."

"Okay." He unlocked the car and then pocketed the keys. "C'mon. Let's search around before we head back."

"If we're lucky, they'll be at the bed-and-breakfast when we arrive."

"I hope they are," said Patrick. "I'll take the left side of the road and you take the right."

We split up. I called out Hannah and Caleb's name as I trudged up the side of the road and then traversed a ditch to go into the forest. I yelled and yelled, but got no response. Even in the fierce wind, the werewolves should've heard Patrick and I shouting their names. Either they weren't around here anymore or they'd already made it back to the bed-and-breakfast. Or maybe they were hiding somewhere hoping to ride out the storm.

But why ditch their car and leave the doors open?

Did something scare them into abandoning their car like that?

I left the forest, using a little vampire flight to avoid splashing into the water sluicing down the ditch. My shoes still came away muddy, and the hem of my jeans were soaked.

I saw Patrick crossing the road to come towards me. Since he didn't have two werewolves in either human or shifter form with him, I assumed he got the same results I did.

Bupkis.

I didn't want to think about the last alternative. Maybe

Hannah and Caleb were lying dead somewhere, the next victims of the murderer.

Maybe we were all on the killer's list because we dared to be at the bed-and-breakfast on the anniversary of the Willescane murders.

Sometimes, this world was all kinds of messed up.

We got back into our car and while Patrick wheeled it around and headed back toward the B&B, I picked forest debris out of my hair.

"Where could they be?" I muttered. I looked out the car window at the burgeoning storm clouds. It hadn't yet started to rain, but I figured it was just a matter of minutes before the deluge began.

"Hey, I see a cell tower," I said. The tall metal tower jutted out of the tree tops, a blinking red light on its top. Lightning lit up the sky and I watched a bright blade of white hit the cell tower. Sparks flew everywhere, and the red light blinked out. Smoke rose from the roasted metal and was whisked away by the crazy wind.

"Holy shit!" My exclamation startled Patrick, and he almost went off the road.

He corrected course, cursing under his breath. "What's wrong, Jess?"

"Lightning hit the cell tower." I took my phone out of my back pocket along with Magistrate Williamson's business card. While I hoped Caleb and Hannah had gone back to the B&B, I had a feeling that they wouldn't be there. I figured calling in the cavalry again might be a good idea. I tried to dial the number, but the call wouldn't go through.

"Great," I said, returning the cell and business card to my back pocket. "The phone service is definitely out."

"Tonight keeps getting better and better."

Less than five minutes later, we pulled into the parking lot. Lilly, Gretta, and Claire waited on the porch for us.

"They abandoned the car at the dock," I said as we got onto the porch and out of the wind. "The doors were opened. They left everything in the car and took off." I looked at their worried faces and knew the answer, but I asked, anyway. "They didn't come back, did they?"

"No," said Lilly.

"Maybe they got stuck somewhere. There are caves and depressions all over the island," said Gretta. "We should at least try to find them before the storm hits."

"We don't have long," said Claire.

"I'll get Duane," said Lilly. "Margaret's too old to be running around the woods in the middle of the night, and Serena is in no condition to be outside. Evan needs to stay with her."

Lilly went inside, presumably to grab Duane.

"We'll each take a section around the house," said Gretta. "Jessica, you and Patrick take the north side—to the graveyard. There's an old garden supply shack near the entrance. It's falling apart, but it's still a decent hiding spot. Claire, you take the garden and search the tree line around the cliff. Be careful. We don't have any barriers. If you slip and fall, you're on a one-way ticket to the ocean."

Duane and Lilly came outside.

"Duane, can you search the woods across from the cottages?" asked Gretta

He looked in the direction that Gretta pointed. I thought he might try to wuss out, but he said, "No problem."

"Thank you."

"Lilly, you and I will go south—from the parking lot and into the woods."

I looked at Gretta. "The cell phone tower is toast. I saw lightning take it out."

"Well, that sucks," said Claire.

"We'll deal with it later. C'mon," said Lilly.

"Wait. I need to let Margaret know what's going on," said Gretta. "I'll meet you out there."

"Okay," said Lilly. "But hurry."

Gretta and Duane went off toward the cottages as Patrick and I headed past the house and into the woods. We called for the werewolves as we darted in and out of the trees, looking under bushes and checking for hidey-holes. We didn't see any of the caves Lilly had spoken about, but it wasn't long before we came upon the cemetery.

The wind blew dead leaves across the ground and their skittering sounded like the rattle of old bones.

"Let's split up," said Patrick.

"You know, every time they do that in Scooby-Doo, Shaggy and Scooby find the masked villain and then there's a lot of running around and screaming."

"Are you saying you're Shaggy?"

"No. I'm saying I'm Scooby-Doo."

He laughed. "So that makes me..."

"Fred. Duh."

He leaned forward and kissed me. "I love you, Jess. Crazy as you are."

"Gee, thanks. Love you, too."

He pointed to the left. "I'll go through there."

"See you in a few."

My husband took off and was soon swallowed by the dark forest. After checking the dilapidated shed and finding nothing inside, I decided to take a quick look at the cemetery.

A rusty wrought-iron fence, most of it leaning inward, surrounded the small graveyard. Seven headstones were visible, but they were crumbling and old, painted with moss and uncared for. When Duane had told the story about the Willescane murders, he'd said that the two younger daughters, the female cousin, the wife Betty, and patriarch Gregory had been killed. But whoever had made the cemetery had included headstones for the missing teenaged daughters, too.

I looked at the names. Gregory. Betty. Jane. Sophia. Heather.

Lilly.

Gretta.

CHAPTER FIFTEEN

Wait. *What?*

I leaned over to study the names on the last two headstones.

Lilly Marie Willescane.

Gretta Janine Willescane.

Holy macaroni. Lilly and Gretta were Willescanes?

Above the whipping wind, I heard the screech of the gate. When I looked to see who'd entered the cemetery, a bright red beam hit my face and blinded me. But not before I saw the ax arcing toward my head.

I scuttled backward as the attacker flashed the red beam at my face again and again while wildly swinging the short-handled blade. With my vampire speed, I zipped to the other side of the cemetery and called for my swords. The instant they appeared in my hands, the killer ran at me faster than should be possible, screaming. I lifted up my blades and crossed them together as the ax swung toward my face.

The person trying to murder me was dressed in black—from the sneakers to the zipped up hoodie. I saw a weird metallic reflection when I tried to look at the killer's eyes.

What the—? The killer yanked the ax off my swords and tried to chop at my ankles. I used one of my blades to sweep away the weapon. It spun across the wet leaves and smacked into Lilly's gravestone.

The next thing I knew, the red light pierced my eyes. Damn it! Blinded, I could no longer see my target. I flailed with my swords, hitting nothing, and then I felt two strong hands shove me backward.

I slammed onto the sagging fence. The red light disappeared, and I watched as the being—person—asshole grabbed the ax and shot out of the cemetery.

I shook off my stupor and started running after the guy.

I took a second to realize that my feet were moving, but I was not.

The ax-wielding jerkface hadn't pushed me away just to escape.

He—or she—had thrown me into the fence. The arrow-tipped rusty spikes lining the top of the wrought iron would be a big problem.

I stared at the metal spike poking out of my belly. I wiggled forward, but moving didn't do much more than increase the size of my wound. It sure didn't free me from being attached to the fence like one of those butterflies pinned inside in a display case.

"Patrick!" I screamed. The wind took my cry and tossed it away. I doubted my husband could hear me even if he was close enough to help.

I wasn't without pain receptors despite being the undead, and I felt a radiating ache in my back.

I was afraid the attacker would come back and finish the job. If he lopped off my head or set me on fire, I would be all the way dead. Panic made me wiggle a lot more but I no matter how I moved, I couldn't remove myself from the pike.

I felt like I was an overturned cockroach trying to flip myself upright again.

I was getting ready to scream my husband's name again when I realized I could reach him by telepathy. Duh, Jessica.

Patrick! Help me!

I waited to hear from my mate, but he didn't respond. And that scared me more than being trapped on the fence waiting for the killer to return and chop me into little pieces.

Patrick. Hello? It's your wife. Your soulmate. Your freaking burden. Someone pushed me onto the cemetery's fence. I can't get off it. Help me!

Once again, there was no response. I felt empty. Like the connection between us lost.

Or dead.

A new panic set it in. Something had happened to Patrick. Either he fell in a hole or found a cave that blocked psychic connections or that ax-wielding maniac had gone after him.

Where was Patrick? Was he okay?

I had no choice. I had to get off this fence and find my husband.

The metal digging into my backside was far more uncomfortable than the rod that had ripped through my organs. I'd already died once before and I didn't like it. I would not end my eternal life stuck on a graveyard fence. Not that I believed I'd still be here when the sun rose. But if I was... *ugh*. I'm ashamed to admit I spent the next few seconds thinking about what my friends in Broken Heart would say. I mean, sure, they'd be sad—at least they better be sad—but you know, at some point, they'd have one of those hushed conversations at the funeral that started with, "She died how?"

Patsy would mention I was a klutz.

No doubt Linda and Eva would chime in on my various klutzy ways. They'd have a good laugh. Nope. I was not going out like this.

"Patrick!"

No response.

Patrick? Honey, are you there? You better mind-call me immediately!

Nothing. Nada. Zip.

"You better be alive," I muttered. "Well, undead. But not dead-dead." Lightning zigzagged across the sky and seconds later, thunder boomed. Cold rain pattered me like tiny icy kisses.

Then I remembered my Get Out of Death card. Or rather the business card of a certain necromancer. I think Mr. Williamson would agree that this was an emergency. I got my phone out of my back pocket and dropped it.

Oh, crap, crap, crap.

Had I dropped the card, too?

I stuck my fingers into my pocket and felt the edges of the card. Yes! I took it out and looked at the words under the telephone number.

"Latin. Great. Why are spells are always in Latin?" I cleared my throat and read, *"Et evocant quibus pythonicus mortuis!"*

I waited for Andrew to appear.

The rain traded ice kisses for hard, cold slaps.

Andrew was noticeably absent. So much for using magical 9-1-1.

Stupid Latin. I looked at the spell again and realized I'd left off the most important part. His name. I tried again. *"Et evocant quibus pythonicus mortuis Andrew Williamson!"*

Silvery Black smoke unfurled in front of me and then disappeared. Andrew stood barefoot, dressed in blue silk striped pajamas, a toothbrush dangling out of his mouth. He looked at me, blinking as the rain pelted him. He stared at me in shock.

"It's an emergency!" I yelled.

"Indeed." He tossed the toothbrush to the ground and spit out his toothpaste. Then he put his arms underneath me and lifted me off the fence.

"Ow!"

"My apologies, Jessica."

"I need blood to heal."

"Or a necromancer," he said. "The dead are kinda my thing." He gently put me on the ground and then placed his palms on the wounds on my stomach and back. He murmured words, Latin probably, and I felt a shock of cold followed by lava-level heat. "There you go. All better?"

When I looked down, I was healed. "Whoa. You're handy to have around."

"Sometimes. What are you doing out here?"

"I routinely throw myself on fences to see if I can Houdini my way off them."

He lifted one eyebrow.

"Everybody needs a hobby," I said. I jumped to my feet. "Caleb and Hannah disappeared. We were trying to find them before the storm hit." I scooped my phone from the pile of wet leaves it had fallen into, stood up, and headed toward the exit. "An ax wielding madman tried to kill me and pushed me onto that fence. And now my husband is missing. I have to find him."

"Where did Mr. O'Halloran go?"

I pointed in the direction I'd seen Patrick take. Then I used my vampire speed to zip through the forest. I got all the way to the cliffs without seeing a single hair of my husband's beautiful head.

"There's a cave over there."

Andrew stood next to me. I looked at him, open-mouthed. "How did you keep up with me?"

"Necromancer, remember?" He waved at me to follow.

We trudged through mud, dead leaves, and other forest

debris as we walked up a slight hill to the cave. All the while, the wind and rain battered at us. You never saw this kind of weather in Jessica Fletcher's Cabot Cove. Sheesh. When we reached the cave, I ducked my head inside and called out, "Patrick?"

I heard a groan.

I had to bend over to get inside, but it a couple feet in, the cave opened up into a bigger space. I could stand up and look around. Andrew was right behind me. I didn't know if his necromancer powers gave him X-ray vision or not. The darkness was thicker than maple syrup, but vampire vision could amplify the minute light. Against the far wall, my husband lay crumbled, moaning in pain.

"Patrick!" I hurried to my husband and put my hand against his head. My fingers came away sticky with blood. "Andrew, hurry!"

The necromancer crouched down, opened his palm and muttered a spell word. A sparkling ball of light appeared, floating upward above Patrick and gave us a better view of the wound.

"Sweet Anubis," said Andrew, appalled at the damage. "It looks like..." He trailed off, studying the injury.

"An ax did this," I said flatly. "Like Julia's wounds, right?"

He glanced at me and nodded. "Yes. We determined she died from massive external and internal bleeding caused by the repetitive strikes of a sharp object."

"You mean she was hacked to death with a freaking ax."

"Yes." He put his hand on top of Patrick's skull. "I think he'll need blood along with my magic." I saw puffs of silvery black emit from Andrew's palm and sink into my husband's head.

I pulled up my sleeve and pressed my wrist against Patrick's cold lips. "Drink, babe," I whispered. "Drink."

Relief poured through me as I felt Patrick's fangs pierce

my skin. He drank deeply, to the point I felt weak, but he could have all the blood in my body if it meant he'd heal.

Andrew reached down and pulled my wrist away. Patrick's eyes opened, flashing red, a growl issuing from low in his throat.

"None of that now, Mr. O'Halloran," said Andrew. "You're healed."

Patrick blinked, his eyes returning to their natural silvery gray color. He gingerly touched the top of his head. Then he looked at Andrew. "How did you do that?"

"Necromancer," I answered for him.

"Ah." Patrick straightened. He reached out and caressed my cheek. "Are you all right, Jessica?"

"Yeah. Thanks to Andrew. Someone tried to remove my face with an ax then they pushed me onto the metal spikes of the fence. I got stuck."

"What?" He looked down at the hole in my shirt and touched my stomach. "I'll rip out the guts of the one who hurt you."

"Not if I get to him—or her—first." I leaned my forehead against his. "I couldn't reach you. I was so scared I'd lost you."

"I'm okay, love." He kissed me. "I'm okay."

"You better be, mister," I said without any heat. "What happened?"

"I'm not sure. I'm calling out for Hannah and Caleb. Next thing I know my head feels like it's been bloody cleaved in two. I checked out this cave earlier and was headed back to you. When I got walloped, the first thing I thought of was the cave, so I zapped myself away from the attack."

"Dang it. Why didn't I think of zapping myself out of harm's way?"

"You called Mr. Williamson, which was the better choice," said Patrick. "I don't think the killer's done yet."

"I agree." Andrew stood up. "I'm going home to get properly dressed and then I'll return. I'll meet you both at the bed-and-breakfast in, say, half an hour."

"Okay," I said.

Andrew left in another puff of black smoke. As soon as he disappeared, so did his ball of light.

I helped my husband to his feet and then hugged him. "Well," I said, pulling back to look at his face. "How do you like our vacation so far?"

Patrick laughed. "It's slightly better than my visit to Pompeii, right before the volcano erupted."

"That's something, I guess."

We held hands as we walked toward the exit of the cave.

"Oh, hey. Guess what I found in the cemetery?"

"Tombstones?"

"Seven, to be exact. Five for the victims who died in the house and two for the teenaged daughters who were never found." I paused. "Lilly and Gretta Willescane."

Patrick whirled me around and looked into my eyes, his expression one of shock. "You're kidding me."

"Nope."

"Why wouldn't they tell us they were the missing daughters?"

"Like you said. Everyone has secrets they want to keep."

And someone wanted to keep his or her secrets bad enough to kill anyone who got too close. Was that why Julia died? And had I been attacked because I'd discovered Lilly and Gretta's secret?

CHAPTER SIXTEEN

*P*atrick and I translocated into the foyer of the bed-and-breakfast. We were both weak, and I no longer cared if Duane knew we were vampires. I could glamour that information right out of his head.

Behind us, the front door opened. Claire and Lilly spilled inside, shutting the door against the storm. They were both soaked to the skin. Neither woman wore black like the person who'd tried to slice off my head, but clothes were easily discarded. Mud spattered their shoes and legs, but I could sniff blood a mile away and there wasn't any on them.

Still, I didn't trust anyone who wasn't Patrick.

Lilly used her vampire speed to disappear and when she returned, she had a stack of towels. She handed them out, and we all dried off.

"No luck?" I asked.

They both shook their heads.

"We didn't even get a whiff of werewolves," I said. "Where could they be?"

"I hope they found a place to hole up and wait out the storm," said Claire.

"Me, too," said Lilly. She looked at us. "Have you seen Gretta?"

"No, but we only got here about a minute before you did," I said. I paused then admitted, "We had a not-so-friendly visit from the Axeman."

"What?" Lilly's eyes went wide. "Are you serious?"

"Deadly serious," I said, putting my towel onto the bench. "I got pushed onto the cemetery fence. Spike went right through my stomach. And then Patrick got slammed in the head with an ax."

"That's insane. Who's running around the island trying to kill everyone? I don't get it." Claire looked us over, her expression concerned. "That's a lot of trauma for vampires. You two need more blood."

"Let's go to the kitchen." Lilly led the way. She opened the fridge and pulled out an IV bag full of blood. "That's weird. I thought we had two left." She turned and handed the bag to Patrick. "Sorry. You must share."

"You first," I insisted when Patrick tried to hand the bag to me. "You got an ax to the skull."

Patrick nodded, ripped off a corner, and drained half the blood. He handed the rest to me, and I choked it down. Bagged blood tastes like drinking expired soup with metal shavings in it. It's not as good as fresh-from-the-carotid-artery deliciousness, but it'll do in a pinch.

Lilly took the bag from me to dispose of and Patrick found napkins so we could wipe our mouths.

"Thanks," I said. I looked at my husband. "Feel better?"

"Yes," he said. "You?"

"Like drinking a Jolt cola."

"Hey." Duane entered the kitchen. His clothes were dry—so I figured he must've gotten back before the storm hit. "I heard you come in. I was upstairs in my room writing out some notes. No sign of Hannah or

Caleb." He studied our faces. "I guess you didn't find them, either."

Was that guilt flashing in his eyes? Why did I have the feeling that Duane barely took the time to look for our missing newlyweds? Like maybe he dashed into the woods, waiting for us all to take off, and then returned to the house.

Oh. Em. Gee.

I bet that weasel came back to search for the hidden room. Everyone was out of the house except Evan and Serena, who were tucked away in Claire's room.

I'd bet a lifetime supply of Godiva chocolate that's exactly what he did. He wasn't putting off a vibe of concealed excitement, so maybe he hadn't found what he was looking for. I hope he hadn't. If the man couldn't put aside his ambition for an hour to find two missing kids, he deserved a whole heaping lot of failure.

"Duane, you didn't see Gretta, did you?" asked Lilly.

He shook his head. "She wasn't here when I got back and I don't think she came in."

"I need to find her."

"You want help?" I asked.

Lilly shook her head. "I'm sure she's around here somewhere."

"Hello, everyone," said Andrew as he walked into the kitchen. He had his trench coat folded over his arm and held his fedora.

"Where did you come from?" asked Duane, surprise on his face.

"The foyer." Andrew swept the room. "No sign of Hannah or Caleb?"

Claire frowned. "How did you—"

"I called him," I said.

"But the cell tower is down," pointed out Duane.

Oops. Dang it. I forgot about the human. "Maybe not," I

hedged. "The call went through." Not a lie. I called Andrew. With a spell. I watched Duane take his phone from his pants pocket and look at the screen. He shook his head. "No bars for me."

"Where is everyone else?" asked Andrew.

"Evan and Serena are upstairs," stated Claire. "Margaret's in her cottage. Gretta is..." She trailed off. "Well, we don't know where she is."

"Another person missing?" Andrew glanced at me, suspicion in his eyes. He lifted an eyebrow. "And where was Gretta when Mr. and Mrs. O'Halloran were attacked?"

Lilly burst out with, "Gretta wouldn't hurt a fly! She wouldn't try to kill anyone—certainly not Patrick and Jessica. And not Julia, either."

"Someone tried to kill you?" asked Duane. He didn't sound surprised—or even upset. Just coldly curious. The writer was, as my mom might say, an odd duck.

"It could've been you," I said.

He reared back as though I'd punched him. "Me? Why would I want to kill you?" He glanced at Patrick. "Or you?"

"Maybe you're the Axeman," I accused. "I mean, not *the* Axeman, but like a copy cat. You said tonight was the anniversary of the Willescane murders. Maybe you're celebrating with a kill-everyone party."

"That's insane."

"So is writing about ax murderers!" I said with a raised voice. Patrick wrapped his arm around my shoulders to keep me from advancing on Duane. I lifted a finger at the writer and let loose with my suspicion. "You knew Julia Davenport."

"I-I did not."

"Yes, you did," confirmed Andrew. "My team and I have spent much of this evening researching everyone's pasts and their connections to the victim. Do you want to admit to it now, Mr. Cutter? Or shall I tell your story?"

Duane gritted his teeth. "Fine. Yes, I knew Julia Davenport. We hooked up a few months ago. A one-night stand, okay? Told me her daughter had gotten knocked up, and she was looking for a place she could hole up until the kid was born."

"You told her about Willescane Island?" asked Andrew.

"I knew about Willescane Island from my research into ax murders. I've been tracking the pattern of a serial killer I believed traveled the country. What happened to the Willescane family fit into the timeline. I'd been trying for months to get on this island. No one in Bar Harbor would help me. Finding any information online about the owners had been futile. But somehow, some way, Julia was able to book a room. She gave me the website info."

Well, that explained how a human found the Thompson Twins' booking site and got a reservation. Duane seemed unaware he'd walked into the parakind world. I now doubted he even knew Julia was a witch.

"So you were stalking Julia, Mr. Cutter?" asked Andrew.

"No!" He huffed out an outraged breath. "I wanted to be here on the anniversary of the family's deaths—for my book. I didn't know Julia and Serena would be here, too."

"I bet she was super thrilled to see you," I said.

"She pretended not to know me, which suited me fine." Duane met Andrew's gaze head-on. "I didn't kill her."

"Perhaps." Andrew turned and looked at Claire. "And what about you, Dr. Woodson?"

"What about me?" She leaned against the counter and clasped her hands together.

"How were you getting paid by Julia?"

Claire's gaze flickered with fear. "The usual way," she said.

"Ah, yes. If you think blackmail is the usual way."

I could see the struggle on Claire's face as she tried to

maintain her composure. "What's between me and my patients is none of your concern."

"Serena is your patient. What Julia said or did doesn't fall under patient confidentiality."

Claire looked down at her hands. "I got out of the curse-casting business after what happened." She returned her gaze to Andrew. "I was in college. Barely twenty. Still training."

"But the young man died." Andrew looked around. "Why don't you tell us why you don't cast curses anymore?"

At first, Claire said nothing. I don't know why Andrew expected her to confess her sins in front of a bunch of strangers. Maybe it was a tactic he used to elicit information. Even so, it was a crappy thing to do. Claire inhaled a deep breath and blew it out slowly. "A friend of mine came to me. She tried to break-up with her boyfriend and he beat her senseless. She asked for my help." Claire hesitated, pressing her trembling lips together as she gathered courage. "I cursed him. The next day, he walked in front of an oncoming train."

"Holy crap," I said.

"That's not the worst part, though, is it?" Andrew's voice was soft with sympathy.

Guilt crowded into Claire's eyes. "She lied to me. He'd broken up with her weeks before she came to me. She'd been stalking him and making his life hell. And she used me to do her dirty work. I let my anger for her and my self-righteousness act as guides to craft a curse he didn't deserve. I ended the life of a good person. After that, I swore I would never cast curses again." She lifted her chin. "And I haven't."

What happened was terrible, but I could hardly fault Claire for trying to help her friend. She looked shaken-up, and I could see the remorse in her eyes. That was a mistake she could never, ever undo. "Are you saying Julia found out about what happened and blackmailed you to take care of Serena?" I asked.

Claire nodded.

The evil Julia perpetuated on those around her was unbelievable. "How did Julia find out?"

"She has—had a lot of powerful friends. She could dig up dirt on anyone." She pressed her palms against her face and sighed. "Julia's wealthy. She could've just paid me. But it gave her sick pleasure to hold that tragedy over my head. She knew if what I did fifteen years ago got out to my patients, it would ruin me." Claire put her arms down at her sides and sagged against the counter. "My life's purpose is to ease the suffering of others. Julia's was hurting everyone she could." She looked up at us, despair in her eyes. "I've never met a meaner soul than Julia Davenport."

I agreed with the doctor's assessment. But blackmail was an excellent motive for murder. Still, she shared the story with us, however reluctantly, so now more people knew her secret. Julia had taken that awful mistake and turned it against Claire. Maybe Claire had killed her to not to only be free of the blackmail—but also to rid the world of the hateful witch. Julia's death would ease the suffering of many people, including Serena.

Claire turned her gaze to Andrew. "Are you satisfied with my humiliation, Magistrate Williamson?"

"Secrets are burdens that get heavier with time. They chain us to the past and to fear. I did not intend to humiliate you, Dr. Woodson. Don't you think it's time you free yourself from your burden?"

Claire seemed to consider his words and then gave a short nod. "I suppose you're right."

"Lilly," said Andrew. "What about you?"

"I'll tell you whatever you want as soon as we find Gretta," said Lilly. "It'll be dawn in a few hours. I'm worried. What if she was attacked, too?"

"A possibility," admitted Andrew. "But sending more people out into that vicious storm risks more lives."

"She's my sister!" Lilly, distraught, strode out of the kitchen. A minute later, we heard the front door slam. Where was she going? Did she suspect where Gretta might be?

"That's not good," said Claire. "We already have three people gone. Now, a fourth."

"What do we do?" I asked no one in particular.

"We wait," said Andrew. "Once the storm passes, we'll do another search for all. Meanwhile, everyone else should stay here."

We heard a crack of thunder that about burst my eardrums. The lights flickered.

And then they went out.

CHAPTER SEVENTEEN

We stood in the dark for a few seconds before I heard Duane say, "We need flashlights."

"We also need to find the breaker box," said Patrick.

"Does anyone know where either of those things are?" asked Andrew.

"I do," said Duane. "I... uh, took a stroll around the house earlier. It's downstairs."

A-ha! I was right. Duane had been trying to find that hidden room—if there was one. That was all supposition on his part. He might be totally wrong about Willescane Island being a smuggling spot for the Vinetta crime family. I suspected he was wrong about his serial killer on a cross-country rampage theory. However, Duane seemed to like his own theories over actual facts.

"Let's find flashlights and get to the breaker box," said Andrew.

"I'll go," said Patrick. Like me, he could see perfectly well in the dark. I figured that Andrew would not use his magic lights because Duane, the human, might freak out. Although maybe blanking Duane's memory of this entire weekend would be a good thing for all of us. Patrick gave me a peck on the cheek and I saw gold sparkles as he magicked himself downstairs.

"What were those sparks?" asked Duane.

"What?" I pretended complete ignorance.

"I didn't see anything, either," chimed in Andrew.

"Must just be you, Duane," added Claire.

I swallowed a laugh. Poor Duane.

A high-pitched scream tore through the house.

I'd heard that kind of scream before—from my own lips when I was in labor.

"It's the ax killer!" yelled Duane. He stumbled across the kitchen and crouched down by the kitchen island. Fear rolled off him in waves. I had a difficult time believing Duane would kill Julia given his level of terror right now.

Another scream echoed down the stairs.

Andrew spun on his heel, but I grabbed him by the arm and stilled his progress.

"It's Serena," said Claire, confirming my supposition. "Her labor might be starting."

"Starting? It sounds more like the final get-this-baby-out-of-me scream," I said.

"I need to get upstairs," said Claire. "I can't see a damned thing."

"Here." I grabbed Claire's hand and led her toward the kitchen's exit.

"Are you sure?" asked Andrew. "It sounds like someone getting murdered."

"You ever push a bowling ball out of your ass?" asked Claire.

"No," said Andrew, sounding taken aback. "Nor would I."

"That's what having a baby feels like. Believe me, you'd scream, too."

"Good lord. If you don't mind, ladies, Duane and I shall wait for Patrick," said Andrew.

"Wonderful," muttered Duane.

"Would you prefer delivering a baby?" I asked as we walked by him.

He didn't respond, so I took his silence for a big, fat no.

I led Claire up the stairs. As we rounded the first landing, Evan burst out of the room. "Her water broke!"

"It's okay," said Claire in a measured, professional tone. "That's normal."

"We need light," I said. "Surely they have candles around here."

As we got to the room, the lights came on. I grinned. "Patrick saves the day."

"Excellent," said Claire.

We found Serena on the bed, sweating heavily, her face a mask of pain. I could see the quilts wet with amniotic fluid and blood. Evan looked unnerved by his girlfriend's level of pain. He was gray—and I thought the kid might pass out.

"We need to get her jeans and panties off," said Claire.

Claire hurried to Serena and put her hands on the girl's belly while Evan and I helped the girl wiggle off her underclothing.

"The baby's turned." Claire checked to see how far along Serena was dilated. "Whoa. She's already at a ten." She glanced up at Serena. "How long have you been in labor?"

Serena shook her head, gritting her teeth, in the throes of another contraction. Claire turned her gaze to Evan. The color was returning to his face. "How long has she been in pain?"

"All day."

"Why didn't you tell me?"

"She didn't think she was in labor," he said. "She thought it was Braxton Hicks contractions."

I'd had false contractions during the later stages of my pregnancy, so I knew full well what that felt like. But for me, there was no mistaking real labor pains for the mild cramping associated with Braxton Hicks. Worry brewed in my gut. So much could go wrong with childbirth in a hospital. And here we were in a bed-and-breakfast without drugs or machines or nurses.

"I have to push," said Serena, panting.

"Not yet." Claire lifted Serena up by the shoulders. "We don't have time to get the bath run, so we're doing this right here and right now, honey. You need to kneel on the bed."

"Kneel on the bed?" I asked. "Are you kidding me?"

"Kneeling or squatting shortens labor and makes giving birth a lot easier." We helped Serena up and held onto her while she got into a kneeling position. She was using Lamaze breathing as she suffered through each contraction. I could feel my womb tighten with sympathy pain. Man alive. That girl was a champ.

"Stop looking so worried, Jessica," said Claire. "This is how women had babies until King Louis the Fourteenth of France. He liked seeing his kids born, so made his wives and mistresses give birth in seated, reclining positions. Before that, women squatted, kneeled or used birthing chairs."

"So the way we give birth now is the result of royal misogyny?"

"Yep."

"What do we do?" asked Evan. He sounded panicked, but at least he was keeping it together. "Be her support. Hold on tight." He got on the other side of the bed and held onto his girlfriend. I grabbed Serena's other side. Claire moved to the front of Serena and checked her.

"The baby's already crowning."

"I gotta push," cried Serena.

"Go for it," said Claire.

Serena scrunched her face and grunted. She gripped my shoulder with the strength of a titan as she bore down, trying to bring her daughter into the world. Claire reached between the girl's legs. "Head's out. Good job. Now breathe."

Some folks might say this was a magical moment, but it wasn't. It was scary and stressful, especially for a girl giving birth without painkillers, an ob-gyn, or a trained pediatric medical crew.

I was freaking out.

But Serena wasn't.

She kept her death grip on my shoulder as she gave another hard push, screaming screamed as the baby's shoulders slipped through.

"One more, Serena," said Claire in an urgent voice. "Just one more push, and you can hold your baby girl."

Serena gave it her all and yelled in relief as the baby slid all the way out and into Claire's arms. The little girl gave a scream that would do a banshee proud.

"Is she okay?" asked Serena, her face red and streaked with tears.

"Better than okay," said Claire. "Jessica, see those clean towels on the nightstand? Get me one, please. Evan, help Serena lie down.

I handed Claire a soft white towel and watched as she efficiently wiped off the tiny infant. Claire put the baby onto Serena's chest. Evan sat down next to his girlfriend, tears in his eyes as he looked at his child. "She's beautiful."

"She is," whispered Serena.

I felt uncomfortable sharing this moment. I was glad to help, glad to see that Serena through the birth of her daughter, but I no longer belonged in the room. While Claire finished her midwife duties and Evan and Serena bonded over their child, I left and closed the door behind me.

What a night.

And it wasn't over.

How could it be with four missing people and a killer who hadn't been caught?

I got to the top of the stairs and saw Patrick on his way up. I moved aside so he could stand on the landing with me. He drew me into his embrace. "How's Serena?"

"Momma and baby are doing great. Daddy's not doing too bad, either."

"That's good." He squeezed me tight, and I squeezed back. Hugs were good medicine. "Jess, this is the craziest vacation I've ever been on."

Considering he was 4,000 years old, I think that was saying a lot. He'd been to a lot of crazy places during crazy times in history. I'd had my fair share of insane stuff, too, but I had to admit, this weekend beat all them—including that time we used a zombie army to fight off threat to Broken Heart.

"I'm worried about Margaret," I said. "She's all alone in that cottage. What if our ax killer took a whack at her?"

"Then let's check on her," he said. "Just to be sure."

We told Andrew we wanted to pop by Margaret's cottage and see if she was okay. He agreed. He and Duane stayed in the parlor near the hearth where the fire offered nice, warm heat. Patrick and I exited out the back porch, away from Duane's prying eyes and deepening suspicions.

Since I'd been to Margaret's before, Patrick and I held hands as I pictured the front porch of the older lady's quaint little house. We sparkled away and within seconds we were at Margaret's door. The cottage was dark, the rain smacking the house and tapping on the windows. I assumed that Margaret must be asleep. At least I hoped so.

"I feel bad about waking her up," I said. "You know, if she's not dead."

"It's better that we check on her," said Patrick. "Especially with all the terrible things happening tonight."

"You're right."

I knocked. We waited as the wind gusted unmercifully against our backsides. The longer time passed, the more worried I got. If I had to, I would pop into the living room and sneak into her bedroom. The idea reminded me of how I used to check on my children at night. No matter how old they were, I would always go into their rooms and put my hand on their backs to feel them breathe. I felt like I should do the same for Margaret. I liked her and wanted her to be okay.

"She's not answering," I said. "Do you think we should go in?

"If we have to," said Patrick.

I knocked again as loud and as hard as I could. Another minute or two passed even though it felt like hours. I was about ready to tell Patrick that we needed to do a little vampire breaking and entering when the porch light flicked on. I heard the snick of the lock turning and then the door cracked open. I saw Margaret peek out.

"What's wrong?" she asked.

I supposed getting vampire visitors at two in the morning merited that kind of question.

"We wanted to see if you were okay."

"Why on Earth wouldn't I be okay?"

"We've had some... er, events in the last hour or so," said Patrick. "May we come in?"

Margaret looked less than thrilled to entertain visitors, and I couldn't blame her. Reluctantly, she opened the door the rest of the way and allowed us inside. She turned on the living room light and then stood near the hearth with her arms crossed. She looked tired although why wouldn't she? We'd just roused her out of bed.

"What's happened? Is everyone okay?"

"Well, we don't know," answered Patrick. "It seems Gretta is gone, too."

Margaret frowned. "What do you mean too?

She didn't appear to know that Caleb and Hannah were missing. Which was weird because I thought Gretta would've told her when she came to check on Margaret earlier.

"Didn't Gretta drop by?" I asked.

"No, dear." She shook her head. "Maybe she knocked and I didn't hear her."

"You heard us."

"I was in the bathroom," she said sheepishly. "Old lady bladder."

"Oh." I cleared my throat. "Caleb and Hanna went missing earlier. Gretta said she was coming by to check on you."

Margaret frowned. "She didn't come by here at all. And now you say she's missing, too?"

I glanced at my husband. *Didn't Lilly say she lost Gretta in the forest?*

Yes.

Then why would Gretta say she's checking on Margaret and not do it?

Maybe she did and Margaret didn't open the door. Like she said, she probably didn't hear Gretta knocking.

"Lilly went to find Gretta," I told Margaret. "So I guess we need to count her among the missing."

"What could she be thinking? Going out in the storm like this?" Margaret tsked and shook her head. "Foolish girl."

"Maybe you should come stay inside the main house," I said. "Patrick and I were attacked earlier and we're worried about your safety."

"Attacked! Someone tried to kill you, too?" Margaret sat down in the recliner and pressed a hand against her chest.

"What on earth is happening?" she asked. "Miss Davenport dying horribly. People missing all over the place. You two getting attacked. It's like a Stephen King novel out here."

"That's what we get for coming to Maine," said Patrick.

"Yeah. We were hoping for Cabot Cove, not Castle Rock," I said.

The rusty tangy of blood assailed my nostrils. It was slight. Barely a scent. But vampires could spot blood easily—especially with our heightened sense of smell. I looked around the room and saw nothing out of place and nothing with blood spattered on it. My gaze moved to Margaret and that's when I spotted the pea-sized spot of blood on the hem of her nightgown.

"Are you all right?" I asked. "You have blood on your nightie."

Margaret look down and squinted, seeing the blood. She shook her head. "Oh my goodness. I cut myself earlier in the bathroom." She looked at Patrick and winked audaciously at him. "Lady things, don't you know."

I thought Patrick might blush with embarrassment. If vampires blushed.

"What about coming back with us?" I asked.

"You know what? I think I will go with you," said Margaret. "I have to admit that I don't feel safe here."

"Patrick, will you take Margaret back to the house?"

"Where are you going?"

"I'm going to check out the second cottage. Maybe Gretta ducked in there to wait out the storm."

"Don't take too long, love."

"I won't."

We waited for Margaret to change clothes and gather her things. When she returned from the bedroom, she had her little cloth tote bag with yarn and a paperback sticking out of the top. She'd exchanged the nightgown for a red- checkered muumuu, her knee-length white socks, and those adorable bunny slippers.

"Have you traveled by vampire before, Margaret?" asked Patrick.

Margaret's smile dimmed. "I can't say that I have."

"You'll be fine," I said. I nodded at them. "I'll be right along."

Before Margaret could form a protest, Patrick hugged her and they disappeared in an explosion of gold sparkles. It looked like a bunch of frenzied fireflies. I locked the door behind me as I left the cottage.

I turned and looked to my right and saw a light on in the second cottage. My hopes rose. Maybe Gretta was in there. And if I was lucky, Lilly would be there too. And if I was really, *really* lucky. I would find Caleb and Hanna huddled in there as well.

But nobody was that lucky.

CHAPTER EIGHTEEN

I zapped myself to the porch and knocked on the door. "Gretta? Lilly?"

I heard a noise and realized someone was moving around in the cottage.

I knocked again. "Who's in there? Hannah? Caleb? Anyone?"

I heard a scraping sound and what I thought sounded like a sob.

I didn't bother knocking again. If the killer was in there, I was gonna kick that jerk's butt. I was ready to rip the door off its hinges, but for the heck of it, I tried the doorknob first. Whaddaya know. The knob turned, and I entered. It was much bigger than Margaret's place, but I didn't have time to study the interior because I spotted Lilly right away.

The small foyer led into the living room. There was a big space between the hearth and the rectangular glass coffee table. As I walked into the living room, I saw that the fire in the hearth appeared to have new logs in it—as if someone had added more wood and stoked it into a nice, roaring fire.

Lilly stood over a pile of ash, an ax in her hand.

Her gaze was full of ghosts and grief when she looked at me, and then she returned to staring at the ashes. When vampires died, their bodies disintegrated leaving nothing but corpse dust. I had to assume I was looking at what was left of Gretta Willescane. Oh, no. No. Not Gretta. I saw the glint of a silver object. As I focused in on it I realized it was Gretta's necklace—the silver filigree with the four birthstones. The one that had belonged to her mother.

I swallowed hard, overcome with sorrow.

Gretta was dead.

And her own sister had killed her.

Lilly looked at me, her eyes glazed over, and lifted the short-handled ax. She showed me the blood smearing the sharp blade. "I found this next to her." She used the ax to point to the right of the fireplace. I saw another smaller pile of ash and realized what had happened.

Gretta's neck had been separated from her body. No doubt with the ax Lilly still held in her hand.

"It's Gretta." She choked on a dry sob. "See that? Our mother's necklace? She never took it off."

It wasn't a confession, but it was close. "Why don't you put down the ax?"

Lilly looked as if she might do it—let the ax fall to the ground. Instead, she gripped it harder.

"Do you know where Hannah and Caleb are?"

She looked at me, her eyes dazed. "You think I hurt them?"

"Did you?"

She shook her head. "Where are your swords?" she asked, her voice a quivering whisper.

"Right here." I lifted my hands and made my swords appear. I swung them in tight arcs. "Just put down the ax, Lilly."

"Not until you say you believe me. I didn't kill my sister."

"But you killed Julia, right?"

"No. As much as she deserved it. Julia was just like my father. Ashamed of her daughter. Mean and vile and vengeful." Lilly's eyes had a wild look to them. "I was in love with Sean O'Malley. To my core. I got pregnant. We were going to get married, but I was only sixteen, and I needed my father's approval. You're not gonna marry a Mick, Lilly." Rage filled her expression, twisting her face as she continued, "Like we were so superior. Daddy's parents got off the boat at Ellis Island same as Sean's grandparents. But my father was so mortified that his daughter was carrying an Irishman's baby. Daddy worked for the mob, but he was ashamed of me. You know what? I was ashamed of him. What he did. Who he was."

"I'm sorry," I said. "I truly am."

But Lilly was lost in her memories. I recalled what Gretta had said to her earlier. *It's set you off again, hasn't it? It's been decades, Lil. Can't you let it go?* Had Lilly's personal tragedy caused a mental breakdown in the past? Had Gretta been worried her sister might go off the rails again?

"You and Gretta are Willescanes," I said. "You lived here in the 1920s."

"Yes," she said softly. "We are—were Willescanes. Daddy moved everyone out to this island so I could have the baby without anybody knowing. Then he took my daughter from me. Ripped her right out of my arms and sent her off to be adopted." She looked at me. "I was going to name her Katherine, after Sean's ma. She was such a lovely woman. Kind and soft-spoken. So unlike my own mother." Her fangs flashed as her anger returned in full force. "Mother was a limp rag. Did whatever Daddy said. She'd rather drown herself in booze than deal with reality."

I felt like Lilly was slipping away—falling further into her past, into her pain. I didn't want to use my swords, and I hoped I could talk her into tossing away her weapon.

Patrick! I sent out to my husband. You better hightail it over here. Lilly's standing over her sister's ashes. With an ax.

Shite! On my way.

I knew Patrick hadn't been in this cottage so I didn't think he'd be able to translocate directly here. I figured I had to keep Lilly busy until he arrived.

"What happened to you?" I asked. "After the baby was born?"

She looked at me, her gaze unfocused. "Daddy was a vampire. The Vinettas did that to him. To a lot of their men. He was Turned about six months after my youngest sister was born. He liked it. Used his powers to control and to hurt. And you know what he did? After I had my child?"

I had a sickening feeling I knew exactly what he did, but I asked anyway. "What did he do?"

"Turned me into a vampire. So I could never get pregnant again. Gretta insisted that he Turn her, too. So I wouldn't be alone." Lilly delved further into her memories, and, I feared, further into madness. "I found out later that Daddy had Sean and his whole family killed. He had five siblings. Two hardworking parents. And his dad's grandparents lived with them, too. That house was full of sunshine and laughter. And love. So much love." Grief washed away her fury, and I saw her grip lighten on the ax. It slid down her fingers until she held the end of the handle. "All of them gone in a spray of bullets."

"Is that why you killed your father? And the rest of your family?"

Lilly looked up at me, her brow furrowing. "You don't know anything." She dropped the ax and fell to her knees, inches away from the hearth.

I'd been so focused on the ax in her hand I hadn't seen what she held in the other. A metal container of lighter fluid.

She squirted herself with the fluid while reaching for the fire just inches away. "Everyone I love is gone," she said.

"No, Lilly!" I cried. I disappeared my swords and dashed through Gretta's ashes trying to get Lilly before she did the unthinkable.

"There's no point to life without love," she whispered. "Remember that." She stuck her arm into the fire.

I grabbed for her shoulder, but the flames licked over her clothing so quickly, that I couldn't touch her.

Not without incinerating myself.

I flung myself away and watched helplessly as Lilly went up in flames. She didn't scream. She didn't move. She let herself be taken by the fire.

She burned.

She burned until she was nothing.

Nothing but ash and bones and memories.

The door to the cottage burst open and the next thing I knew, Patrick was scooping me into his arms and dashing out the door. In the blink of an eye, he'd returned us to the back porch. Andrew waited there, his gaze unreadable.

"The cottage is on fire," said Andrew.

"Gretta's dead," I said as I pulled away from my husband's comfort. "And Lilly covered herself in lighter fluid and set herself ablaze." Horror and grief choked my voice.

Silent and sorrowful, we turned and watched as fire burst through the windows and poked up through the roof. It didn't last long, however. The sheets of endless, icy rain and roaring wind soon extinguished the flames.

"Lilly and Gretta were the missing Willescane daughters," I said to Andrew. "She had a kid and her dad took it away. Then he Turned her and her sister into vampires." I shook my head sadly. "She blamed her whole family. Even Gretta. I think she snapped."

"She killed Gretta?" asked Andrew.

"Sure looked like it. And she probably killed Julia to protect Serena." I turned to Andrew. "I think she killed the whole Willescane family in 1926, too," I said. "Her father Turned her, she killed everyone, and Gretta took her away."

"Why would they come back here?" asked Patrick.

"To heal the wounds of the past, maybe," said Andrew.

I harrumphed. "Well, that sure as hell didn't work out."

"No," he said, looking at the decimated cottage. "It did not."

CHAPTER NINETEEN

We were quiet for a long moment as we watched the storm wipe clean the sins of Willescane Island. My heart hurt for the twins, for Lilly, in particular. Her mental illness had pushed her to do horrible things. And poor Gretta. She'd protected her sister for decades—helping Lilly stave off her demons. It seems not even she could shield Lilly from the past forever although it was obvious she'd tried.

Why would they ever return to this island? To the place where they lost everything?

"What are we going to tell everyone?" I asked Andrew.

"The truth," he said.

"Even Duane?"

Andrew shook his head. "If one of you would be so kind as to glamour the man, we'll forego explanations to him."

"I'll do it," said Patrick. "How much do you want him to forget?"

"Everything," I answered. I glanced at Andrew. "Including any prior knowledge he had. We can't have him writing about the Willescanes or this island. It's time to let that family rest in peace. And we don't need more humans poking around this place. Which is what will happen if Duane publishes a book about the Willescane murders and tries to attach it to his ax-murderer-across-the-nation theory."

"I agree," said Andrew. "I'll ensure that his notes and manuscript disappear off his computer. We'll have to replace his memories with something else."

"We need to do more than that," I said. "We should give him a different direction in his research. I don't want him to step foot in Maine ever again."

"How about Fall River, Massachusetts?" asked Patrick. "Lizzy Borden's parents were killed by an ax murderer."

"Um... didn't Lizzy Borden kill them?" I asked.

"She was acquitted," mused Andrew. "So, yes. It's perfect." He clapped his hand against my husband's shoulder. "Good show, Patrick."

"Sounds like we have a plan. Except... everyone's stuck on this island until at least Monday," I said. "The ferry's DOA and can't be repaired until then."

"No worries, Jessica," reassured Andrew. "I'll make arrangements to get everyone off the island as soon as the weather clears."

We returned to the parlor where Duane, Claire, and Margaret waited for us. Patrick asked to speak to Duane alone, and they went off to the dining room. I let Andrew handle the explanations of what had happened, including the tragic truth that the vampire twin sisters had died, joining their family in the resting place they had left so long ago. It hadn't escaped my notice that Lilly and Gretta had left this earth on the anniversary of their family's murders. Had Lilly planned it that way?

I didn't think so.

I wasn't sure how the others would feel, but I felt like crap about the whole situation. I went into the kitchen and decided to make a pot of tea for everyone. Chamomile was perfect since it was supposed to be calming. I hoped it had a whole lot of calming in it. I wished I could make everyone Xanax tea. That would work a lot better.

But chamomile would have to do.

The ceramic tea set with the gold-rimmed cups had been washed and set out, probably so Gretta could offer guests a nice beverage while they enjoyed the comfort of the parlor.

I had a moment of sharp grief that left me clutching the countertop. Gretta had been such a sweetheart. The memory of Lilly setting herself on fire flashed through my brain. She couldn't live without the sister she'd killed. So she'd joined her.

At least that's what it seemed like on the surface.

A sense of wrongness filled me.

Something felt unfinished. Like the story wasn't over.

No. It wasn't that. More likely, I didn't want it to be over. I wanted a different ending. I remembered the picture in the dining room of the two little girls playing in a field. I realized those must've been the twins' younger sisters. And the tree with the carved initials? *L+S 4ever*. Lilly and Sean. Two lovers who would never have a happily-ever-after.

Just as I pulled the steeper out of the teapot, Patrick entered the kitchen.

"Wow, that was fast," I said. "I take it Duane is reprogrammed?"

He nodded. "There's not even a whisper of Willescane Island in his mind. He's very excited about researching Lizzy Borden and Fall River. I put him to bed, and he'll wake up his own house tomorrow courtesy of the magistrate."

"That's great."

"What are you doing, love?" he asked.

"I feel like I need to take care of something. Or someone. So that's what I'm doing." I put the metal steeper into the sink and rinsed off my hands. "Chamomile. Lilly and Gretta have a lot of loose-leaf teas. I threw some jasmine in there, too." I looked around the kitchen. "It's such a shame."

Patrick leaned down to give me a kiss. "It must have been awful what you saw," he said. "Lilly killing herself like that."

"Awful doesn't cover it," I said. "Awful is stubbing your toe. Awful is not getting the last Ben & Jerry's Chunky Monkey in the freezer. Lilly? What she did was horrifying."

"I guess she couldn't live with herself after killing her sister," said Patrick, echoing my earlier thoughts.

But that wrong feeling came over me again. "She didn't exactly confess," I hedged.

He stared at me. "What are you saying, Jess? That you don't think she killed Gretta or Julia?"

I shrugged. "I don't know what I'm saying. It's just... I feel off about the whole thing." I re-arranged the teacups on the silver tray. "It probably makes the most sense that Lilly lost her mind after watching the way Julia treated Serena. So, she kills Julia the same way she offed her family." I couldn't wrap my brain around one fact though. "Gretta told their father to Turn her, too. She sacrificed her mortal life to make sure Lilly wouldn't be alone in her eternal one."

"Somewhere deep inside," said Patrick. "Lilly blamed Gretta the same way she blamed everyone else in the Willescane family for taking away her child."

"Yeah. I guess." I fiddled with the lid of the teapot. "I wonder if Lilly ever tried to find the daughter she would have named Katherine."

"It doesn't matter now, love. She's at rest. The Willescanes are gone."

"But not their island." I glanced at him, an idea growing in my mind. An idea my husband might not be as enthused about. "What do you think will happen to this place?"

He studied my expression. He cupped my cheek, concern

in his gaze as he asked, "You want to take over the bed-and-breakfast, don't you?"

Patrick knew me so well. I wasn't sure I wanted to admit that yes, I really did. Like I said, the idea was both exciting and scary. "Lilly and Gretta just died, so I feel crappy for even thinking about it. I was kinda already contemplating the idea of getting our own island and doing our own kind of B&B. But now..."

"Now you want this one."

"I'm a horrible person."

He drew me into his embrace. "You are not horrible."

"I know how to take care of people. I want a different direction. I know this island has had its share of tragedies but maybe we can create a really special place. We can replace all that bad with good."

"I know you've been looking for something to fill the hole left by the kids growing up," said my husband. "And I know Broken Heart isn't the same after our friends departed town. But do you really want to buy an entire island? And do you really want to run a bed-and-breakfast for the undead?"

"Well, for all of parakind." I touched his arm, looking into his eyes. "It's not just about me. It's about us. Something for us to do together. Maybe it's a little nuts to want to buy an island and run a bed-and-breakfast, especially this one, but I think we could make this place really great. We could build a little town on the island, too. It's big enough for a small supernatural population. Maybe 100 people or so."

"You mean like Broken Heart two point oh?" He asked.

I shook my head. "No. More like a new beginning. I don't know for sure. Broken Heart has gotten so much bigger. And everyone seems a lot busier. There's always new construction going on. We have two schools there, now. Every house is occupied. Downtown is crowded with businesses. I mean, that's all good. It really is."

"But it's not where you want to be anymore," said Patrick.

"No, I don't," I admitted. Relief flowed through me. Until Patrick said the words, I hadn't accepted their truth. I didn't want to be in Broken Heart anymore. And I knew now what had driven my restlessness: My desire to find a new purpose. "How do you feel about that?"

"Home is wherever you are," said Patrick. "If this is what you want then I will find a way to give it to you."

"But what about you? I want you to be happy too."

"I think I could be happy here," he said. "There's a lot to do around this old place. And so much that we can change and make better. I like the idea, Jess. So, let's do it."

"This is why I love you," I said.

"I love you, too, *mo chroí*."

I picked up the tea tray, and we made our way into the parlor. Andrew stood by the hearth, staring at the fire. Margaret sat in one of the wingback chairs, her crochet project untouched in her lap. She looked devastated by the news of Gretta and Lilly's death.

Claire sat forlornly on the love seat. She looked up at us. "I don't think Serena and Evan need to know—at least not right now."

"Good call," I said. "How are they? And the baby?"

"Sleeping," she said. "The baby's already nursed. Healthy girl with a good appetite."

"That's wonderful." I passed out the tea to everyone. The fire crackled, the only sound in the grief-stricken silence, while they sipped tea and tried to process all that had happened on this single, terrible night.

Andrew put his cup on the mantle. "Good cuppa, Jess. Thank you."

"No problem."

"I've checked in with my team and updated them on the situation."

"The phones are working?" I asked.

"No. I used other means."

"Necromancer," said Patrick, smiling.

"Exactly." Andrew flashed a quick smile. "It looks like the storm should pass soon. Clear skies predicted tomorrow morning. We'll move everyone from the island to Bar Harbor. We still have to take statements and examine the crime scene."

"What about Hannah and Caleb?" I asked. "They haven't shown back up. Either they found a hiding spot or..." I couldn't finish the thought. Had Lilly been the one who'd frightened them out of the car? Had she used her ax to cut off their heads? The only sliver of hope I had was that during our search we hadn't found any bodies. I had to believe the newlyweds were alive.

"Do you think they were killed, too?" Claire pressed a hand against her heart as if it might break. I felt that way, too. Like my heart would surely crack open and bleed if anything else bad happened. "I hope not."

"Let's think positively," said Andrew.

"I can't wait to get the hell off this island," muttered Margaret. "It's cursed." She looked around at all of us. "And so is everyone who steps foot on it."

CHAPTER TWENTY

*A*fter finishing her tea, Claire said good night and went upstairs to bed.

"I won't get a wink tonight," said Margaret as she gathered her belongings. She paused and looked at me. "Where should I go? Do you want me to take the couch?"

"I don't think that would be comfortable at all, Margaret. You could take the newlyweds' room," I said. "All the others are occupied."

"I'm not sure my knees can manage all those stairs, dear." She smiled. "The price of aging."

"I'll carry you," said Patrick.

She lifted her hand. "No, thank you. I have some pride left in these old bones."

"How about I magic you up there?"

Margaret shuddered. "I don't think I can take another magical transport. The last one about gave me a heart attack."

There were only ten steps to the basement where the other two rooms were located. It would be easier for the older woman to manage. "What about... er, Lilly and Gretta's room?" I could tell from Margaret's expression she didn't want to stay in the bedroom of her former bosses.

Patrick must've thought the same because he said, "Take our room. We'll sleep in Lilly and Gretta's."

Relief flowed over Margaret's face. "Thank you." She smiled at him. "Now, I won't take a vampire trip through the ether, but I would accept help down those bit of stairs."

"At your service," said Patrick. He held out his arm and Margaret wrapped her gnarled fingers around his forearm.

"Such a gentlemen," she tittered.

Patrick led her toward the back basement staircase, leaving me in the parlor with Andrew. The clock on the mantle ticked away the time while the fire crackled and snapped. Together, the sounds created a soothing tune. This kind of cozy moment was what I wanted for the bed-and-breakfast and the guests who would come here.

"Patrick and I want to take over Willescane Island," I blurted.

Shock registered on his countenance. "My lord."

"I know. It's quick, isn't it?" I pressed my lips together. It was one thing to talk about this crazy plan with my husband, who understood and loved me, and completely different to admit to a new friend what I was thinking especially so soon after the owners had died. And Caleb and Hannah were still missing. Despite everything Lilly had done, I believed her about the werewolves. I don't think she hurt them.

"I don't want the island to fall into the wrong hands," I further explained to Andrew. "I want to do something good with it. We're thinking we could build a small supernatural town here, a sanctuary of sorts."

Andrew's brow furrowed as he considered what I was saying. "Like you did in Broken Heart?"

"Yes," I said. "Although that wasn't me so much as the Consortium vampires."

"Consortium. Yes, I know of them. A parakind organization that works with scientists and intellectuals to better mankind—behind the scenes, as it were." He nodded. "I think it's a good idea, Jessica. Perhaps you and Patrick can create something better on the ashes of these tragedies."

"Yes," I said softly. "I think we can."

"Me, too." He sighed. "I hope Hannah and Caleb are all right. We've had enough death on this terrible night."

"Too much," I said.

"Indeed," said Andrew. "Well, then. I must return to my office," said Andrew. "Tomorrow, the weather should be clear. We'll transport everyone off the island before you and Patrick arise. And hopefully we'll be able to track down the werewolves, too." He paused. "You won't mind being on the island alone for a bit?"

"We'll be dead to the world," I said. "So, no, we won't mind."

He chuckled. "Yes. There is that." He pushed away from the hearth, glancing at the clock on the mantle. "Two hours before dawn. It's been quite the evening, hasn't it?"

"That's the understatement of the century."

He smiled. "Good night, Jessica."

"Good night, Andrew."

The magistrate disappeared in a puff of silvery black smoke. He certainly knew how to make an exit. A couple minutes later, Patrick returned from escorting Margaret to our room and getting her settled in.

"She likes to flirt," he said.

"Well, you are pretty cute."

"Am I?"

"The. Cutest."

He kissed me—the kind of kiss that made me tingle all the way to my toes. After sixteen years of marriage, he still rocked my world.

And he always would.

Together, we picked up the parlor. I washed the tea set and set the cups and teapot in the rack to dry. We both made a final round around the house to make sure it was locked up tight. Even with the ax murderer dead, I still had the jitters. Not for me, but for everyone else, especially the couple and their new baby.

I hoped, too, that Caleb and Hannah were all right. Please, I sent up to the skies to whatever deities might be listening, let those two walk in here safe and sound.

Patrick doused the fire in the parlor's hearth and then we turned off the main lights, leaving on two lamps in the parlor and an additional one in the hallway.

"Hey, Jess. Hear that?" said Patrick cocking his head.

"What?" I listened, but I heard nothing. Oh. I got it. "It stopped raining."

"Ayuh," said Patrick mimicking the Maine accent.

I laughed. "Thank goodness."

Patrick and I headed downstairs. We wouldn't go to sleep right away but we could both use some prime time snuggling and decompressing. Just as we were mid-way down the stairs, we heard a banging on the front door.

"That can't be Andrew," I said. "He just left." I wiggled my fingers. "He knows how to translocate using necromancy magic. Why would he have to knock?"

"Who else could it be?" asked Patrick.

"Oh my God. Do you think it's Hanna and Caleb?

The banging came again, this time harder and more desperate. Patrick and I used vampire speed to get us to the front door within seconds.

My husband unlocked and opened the door. I couldn't believe my eyes. It was like the deities had heard my prayer, and wow, they responded way quicker than I thought they would.

Hanna and Caleb stood at the door holding each other, shivering almost out of their skins. They looked muddy and soaked, but other than that no worse for wear. I wonder why they hadn't shifted. At least I assumed they hadn't. Clothing never transitioned with shifters, so they got naked before taking their animal forms. Given the panicked state in which they'd left their vehicle, I didn't think Hannah and Caleb would've taken the time to discard their clothing before shifting into wolves.

"Come in, come in," I said.

Patrick shut the door behind them. "I'll get the fire started again."

I ushered the couple into the parlor, grabbing two throws off the back of the couch. They wrapped in the thick knit blankets and went to sit in the two wingbacks closest to the hearth.

Patrick had the fire roaring again in no time at all.

"Hang on," I said. "Let me fix you something warm to drink. How about some hot chocolate?"

"That sounds amazing," said Hannah. "Anything to eat? We're starving."

"I'll make you some sandwiches."

I went to the kitchen. The container of cocoa was in the same cabinet stuffed with the jarred loose-leaf teas. While the milk warmed in the microwave, I pulled out homemade wheat bread, thick slices of ham and Swiss cheese, and a container of spicy German mustard. Werewolves were big eaters, and starving werewolves were even bigger eaters, so I made each of them two sandwiches with double meat and double cheese.

I made the hot chocolate, topped it with whipped cream I found in the fridge, and then put the mugs and plates onto a wooden tray sitting on the kitchen's center island.

I hurried into the parlor and put the tray on the little

table in-between the chairs. I watched as Hanna and Caleb grabbed at the food. They inhaled the first sandwiches, and while they ate, Patrick and I gave them the short version of what had happened.

"Lilly and Gretta are really dead?" asked Hannah.

I nodded.

"That sucks," muttered Caleb. "They were nice. For vampires." He glanced at us. "Uh, no offense."

"I think you're nice," I said. "For a werewolf."

He grinned.

"Magistrate Williamson will be here tomorrow to take everyone home." I studied their tired expressions. "Where have you been? We had search parties all over the island trying to find you."

"We... uh, found a cave about halfway up to the B&B," said Hannah. "It started pouring, and it was so cold. Neither one of us had our jackets." She took a big bite of her second sandwich. Caleb took up the story in-between bites of his second sandwich.

"We waited out the storm in the cave," said Caleb.

"Why didn't you shift?" I asked. "You could've made it back in no time flat."

Caleb swallowed the large bite he'd just taken. "We didn't want to show up naked."

"Uh-huh." My mom radar pinged hard. "Shifters don't give a pig's curly tail about nakedness. What are you not telling us?"

Hanna and Caleb share a look. Finally, Caleb caved.

"I wouldn't have believed it if I hadn't seen it with my own eyes," he said, "but there was a ghost."

Hannah nodded. "The ghost of a little girl," she clarified.

"Yeah. Hannah was right. Those murdered little girls are haunting the house."

"You saw more than one?" I asked.

Once again, Hannah and Caleb shared a look. Then Hannah said, "No. Just Sophia."

I felt my body go cold. "Sophia?"

I glanced at Patrick and thought-sent to him, *Sophia's name was on one tombstone. I think she was one of the younger Willescane sisters.*

And here I thought Hannah was being melodramatic, admitted Patrick.

Me, too.

"Sophia showed up in our room," said Caleb.

"You mean Claire's room?"

"Yeah. Weird, right? Because it was supposed to be an old sewing room or something. We thought we got out of the bedroom where the little girls were killed. And then one shows up floating right over us."

I didn't point out that ghosts could appear wherever they wanted. That was the benefit of being a spirit. You weren't chained to anything—corporeal or inanimate.

"We freaked out," said Caleb. "All that talk about the ax murderer and now we're seeing actual ghosts. It was bizarre."

"We just wanted to go home," said Hannah. "We knew Evan had stolen the ferry." She glanced at us sheepishly. "We overheard Gretta tell you about that."

"You thought you could put your car on the ferry and pilot it home in a storm?" asked Patrick, disbelieving.

"A human did it," pointed out Hannah. "How hard could it be?"

"Well, you missed the part where the engine flooded and it needs to be fixed," I said. I stopped myself from pulling out the old parental favorite: If Evan jumped off the Empire State Building, would you do the same? You make your own choices and you never assume you can do something just because someone else does it.

However, Hannah and Caleb were grown-ups. Mostly.

"We never even made it to the dock," said Caleb. He finished his last sandwich and wiped his fingers on a napkin. "Sophia appeared right above our car. She said we were in danger and to run."

"She knew we were werewolves, too," said Hannah.

"At least we think so. She kept telling us 'nice doggie.' It was kinda insulting."

"Oh, Caleb. She's a just a little girl."

"A dead little girl," he muttered.

His wife punched him on the arm. "She saved our lives." Hannah looked at us. "She showed us where the cave was."

"The storm stopped only a few minutes ago," said Patrick. "But you two are soaked to the bone. Did you leave the cave while it was still raining?"

"She told us it was safe to come back here," said Caleb, "and that the danger was over."

"Sophia didn't steer us wrong," added Hannah. "Because Lilly is gone, and she was the killer. Right?"

"Yeah," I said. "Right."

"We're sorry we worried everyone," said Hannah, "but that little girl—she was the real deal."

"I believe you," I said. "You were lucky. And I'm really glad you two are okay."

"We're exhausted." Hannah yawned. "I want a hot shower and then I want to sleep for a while week."

"Go to bed," I said. "Sweet dreams."

"And no visits from ghosts," added Caleb under his breath.

We wished the newlyweds good night. Once again, Patrick put out the fire and turned off the main lights. While he was locking up, I did the dishes.

Patrick and I headed downstairs to bed.

"That's the final mystery solved," said Patrick. "Right?"

I nodded. "Right."

CHAPTER TWENTY-ONE

"This has been the longest night of my unlife," I said as we entered Lilly and Gretta's room.

"It sure feels like that," agreed Patrick. He shut the door behind us and we paused to take in our surroundings. It was smaller than our room. I walked around and opened doors. There were two walk-in closets, one on each side of the room. Inside the closets were make-up tables with little velvet chairs and oval mirrors. The in-suite bathroom had only a garden tub, separate shower, and double-sink, but no toilet. Vampires never went to the bathroom so that made sense.

I have to admit I felt strange standing in Lilly and Gretta's room, about to fall asleep in their beds. They hadn't died in here, but it still felt disrespectful to be in their space.

You could almost see a line drawn down the middle of the room. On each side I saw a twin bed, a nightstand and a dresser. Each woman had her own style. Gretta with her black and brown dresses and flat shoes. Lilly with her red and purple gowns and kitten high heels. Lilly's bed was neatly made, a big yellow quilt tucked in and two fluffy pillows slanted on top. Everything on her dresser was aligned and in its proper place. Her nightstand held only a small yellow-shaded lamp.

Gretta's bed wasn't made at all. Her dresser was a mess of stockings, make-up, and hair accessories. Crowded around the tiny lamp on her nightstand were a paperback, lipstick, butterfly barrettes, and a capped pen.

Patrick drew me into his arms and held me. He always seemed to know when I needed comfort. The way Patrick loved me was unreal. I'd been married before. My first husband was an insurance salesman, and we'd had what I considered a normal life—until he cheated on me and got another woman pregnant. Before I could divorce him, he died in a car wreck. Anyway. Normal, right? But with Patrick, love was different. Better. Solid and pure and beautiful. And as far from normal as you could get. He often called me his *céadsearc*, which in Gaelic translated to "first love." That was a helluva compliment from a man with four millennia under his belt.

"Do you want to push the beds together, Jess?"

"Yes. I don't want to sleep apart from you." We took a few minutes to rearrange the other furniture so we could shove the twin beds together in the middle of the room. When we moved Lilly's bed against Gretta's, I noticed a cut square on the wood floor.

"Hey," I said to my husband. "Look at this."

Patrick rounded the bed and looked down at the floor. On the left side of the square was a handle. Patrick and I looked at the trap door and then at each other.

"Do you think Duane was right about the secret room?" asked Patrick.

"Only one way to find out."

Patrick lifted up the door. We saw the top of a wood

ladder. I crinkled my nose as a foul smell attacked my nostrils. I waved my hand in front of my face. "What is that?"

"Could be anything," said Patrick as he peered down into the dark space below. "Mold. Rotting food. Dead wildlife." He looked at me over his shoulder. "I'll go down first."

"Be careful."

He descended the ladder. A few seconds later, I heard the click of a switch. A dim yellow light appeared.

"Come on down."

I scrambled down the ladder and landed on a concrete floor. The walls were concrete, too. The space wasn't huge—maybe a ten by ten room. Crates, many of them collapsed, lined the walls. Brown and green broken bottle littered the floor. I think they'd fallen out after the wood rotted away and became too weak to hold their cargo anymore.

"So Duane was right about the secret room and the bootlegging," I said.

"I suppose Lilly and Gretta wanted to forget about this place. Proof of what their father had been."

"They didn't need anymore bad memories," I said. "There's the tunnel." I nodded toward the wall behind my husband. "I bet it goes right to the docks."

"I bet you're right."

Once again, I got a whiff of that awful smell. I moved around the room trying to found the source.

"I think it's coming from the tunnel," said Patrick.

"Maybe it's the ocean."

"I don't think so." Patrick turned and started down the tunnel.

I followed him.

He was a few inches over six feet tall, and the top of the tunnel brushed his head. I was surprised he didn't have to bend over. It was wide enough for us to walk side by side even though there was less than five inches of space on either side of us.

More crates and broken bottles lined the walls. The further we walked, the stronger the stench got—and now it was getting mixed with the salty rot rolling in from the ocean.

Ahead I saw what looked like a pile of clothes, but I couldn't say for sure. "Doesn't this tunnel have a light?" I asked.

"Probably not," said Patrick. He pulled out his cell phone he turned on its flashlight setting. He pointed it down the tunnel, but we had to walk forward a few more feet to the lumpy laundry.

Only it wasn't laundry.

It was a body.

A young, overweight man wearing a black button-up shirt tucked into belted khaki pants lay crumpled on the gritty, wet ground.

The end of the tunnel was only two or three feet away. Had he dragged himself in here and died? Of what? Too young for a heart attack or stroke. Maybe asthma or an aneurysm?

"Who is he?" I asked.

Patrick squatted down and rolled him over. With the man now on his back, his cause of death was obvious.

A big, deep gash in his chest.

An ax wound.

I felt bile in the back of my throat. "How awful."

Patrick pointed to a gold name badge attached to his shirt. "Milton," he read. "Day Manager."

"Oh, my God." I stared at the body and remembered Gretta telling us how their previous day manager had disappeared.

But he hadn't stopped showing up because he wanted to quit the job.

Someone had made sure he would never work on Willescane Island again.

"Why would Lilly kill him?" Patrick shook his head. "It doesn't make sense."

"No," I said. "It doesn't." Foreboding clutched my belly. We'd missed something. The sense of wrongness I'd felt after Lilly ended her life returned in full force. "We need to call Andrew."

"Good idea," said Patrick. He handed me his cell phone.

I reached into my back pocket to grab Andrew's business card.

It was gone.

I checked all of my jean pockets. Empty. And I'd left my phone in the room. "Shoot. We have to go back."

"Just as well. I'm not keen to spend any more time with Milton."

"Ditto."

We headed toward the secret room. We hadn't quite gotten to the exit when a figure dressed head-to-toe in black appeared, blocking our way.

This time, however, the attacker hadn't bothered pulling up the hoodie to hide her face this time.

"Margaret," I said. "What are you doing?"

"Trying to finish what my parents started, dear." She twirled the ax with the expertise born of use and practice.

A pair of camouflage night goggles perched on top of her gray curls. I realized those goggles had been the metallic gleam I saw when she'd been in the cemetery trying to kill me. Hidden under her grandmotherly smiles and quaint Maine accent was the real murderer of Willescane Island.

"You killed Gretta," I accused her.

"I had to," she said. "She was a vampire."

"Julia was a witch."

"Killing Julia was an accident. I thought she was Lilly. But then Lilly did the right thing and killed herself. I'll allow you to do the same." She grimaced. "In fact, I'd prefer it. I like you, Jessica. And you, too, Patrick. But you're shells of the humans you once were. You wander the earth in search of something, anything, to fill up the holes where your souls once lived."

"We have our souls," said Patrick. "We're not *droch fola*."

"Droch what?"

"Vampires who've lost their souls," I said. "They don't care who they hurt, but we do. We live in peace in this world."

"Impossible," spat Margaret. "All vampires are the same."

I noticed the blood at the corner of her mouth. "You've been drinking blood. What are you?"

"Human," she said, pride stamped in her tone. "I'm not a vampire, if that's what you're thinking. I would never, ever be one of you filthy creatures."

"I don't think a human on a blood diet should judge us," I said.

"Drinking the blood of vampires is the only thing that gives hunters the speed and strength we need to rid the world of you." She advanced.

"You don't want to do this." I held up my hands as if that might stop her from moving toward us.

"I have a duty. An oath to uphold. And in this case, I had to mete out justice. You see, Jessica, Gregory Willescane murdered my parents." She twirled the ax again. "My parents came here on a mission to kill the bloodsuckers. And they did."

"They killed kids," I said horrified. "Those little girls weren't vampires!"

"It was better for the young ones to die than be raised by the filthy undead. My parents put them out of their misery.

Mom and Dad believed they'd gotten them all, but then Gregory Willescane appeared in the parlor. He ripped out my father's throat. Then he did the same to my mother, but with her last dying breath, she pushed him into the fireplace. He burned to death."

Margaret's voice held gruesome delight.

"If everybody died that night, how do you know Gregory killed your parents?" asked Patrick.

"I was six months old when they died. The members of the Society raised me. When I got old enough, they told me everything. How the twin daughters had escaped. Where the secret room was located. How to get into the tunnel. When I turned sixteen, I became hunter for the Society, too. Just like my parents."

What the heck is the Society? I thought-sent to Patrick.

I don't know. I've never heard of it.

If she was born in 1926, she's ninety-two-years-old.

She doesn't look more than seventy, sent Patrick, *so she's probably drinking vampire blood a lot. It would give her that kind of youth.*

"I served my time. Me and my Harold," said Margaret. "We dispatched vampires and rid those creatures from the earth. Then we retired. Life was good until Harold got cancer and God took him. Then I heard that Lilly and Gretta had returned. Oh, they used the Thompson last name, but I knew it was the Willescane twins. I needed to finish the job that cost my parents their lives." She was within striking distance now, her eyes dilated—no doubt from the vampire blood she'd imbibed before she came to confront us. "And I will kill you both, you dirty, rotten vampires!"

Margaret screamed and ran toward us. I didn't think it would take much for Patrick and I to take down a little old lady, even one high on vampire blood.

Boy, were we wrong.

Margaret was quick and well trained and she swung the ax with an ungodly skill. She nicked us both time and time again as we tried to get away from that deadly blade. She was so fast and so good we spent all of our time defending ourselves.

"Jessica," said Patrick as he avoided another blow from Margaret, "call for your swords!"

CHAPTER TWENTY-TWO

I made my swords appear and fought back against Margaret's swinging ax. She fended off every move I made. My goal was to keep her busy enough for Patrick to get close and take her down. But anytime Patrick tried to get closer to her she would slash it him only to whirl back at me. Her dose of vampire blood gave her the same amount of strength and speed we had, and we lost the advantage we should've had over her.

But then she started to slow down. It became more difficult for her to meet my blows. I guess the vampire blood she'd taken hadn't lasted long enough to kill us. I kept parrying and thrusting, pushing her back toward the secret room.

Patrick shot behind her and grabbed her arm. She yelled and swung around, embedded the ax into his stomach.

He screamed and let go of her, staggering backward.

Margaret crowed in triumph as she leaned down to pull out the weapon. I didn't even give her time to put her fingers on the handle. I used my full weight to shove her away. She cried out, flying down the tunnel. She crashed to the ground hard. And yet, she climbed to her feet and turned to face us once more. Her face was bloody, and she wasn't putting weight on her left ankle.

I did not want to kill her. There had been enough death and tragedy on this island and I would not contribute one more body.

I made my swords disappear. And used my speed to get to Margaret before she could take a single step. I swept her legs out from underneath and she fell back to the ground. She lifted up on her elbows, intending to rise again, but I snap-kicked her in the jaw.

The blow knocked her unconscious. She collapsed, going limp.

I rushed to my husband.

"Shite," said Patrick pulling the ax out of his stomach. "That's going to leave a mark."

"I'll get Claire," I said.

"No time, love. It's almost dawn. Let me have a little blood and I'll heal while we sleep."

Patrick took sustenance from my wrist and soon his wound healed enough for us to leave.

We didn't have a choice about when we passed out. The closer dawn got, the less mobile we became.

But we had to do one thing first.

Patrick took off his torn shirt and ripped it in half. We used one half to tie Margaret's wrists and the other tied to her ankles. She'd stay here wrapped up like a present for the magistrate.

We held onto each other and transported into the bedroom. Patrick shut the trap door. Then we collapsed into the bed and within seconds, we both fell into unconsciousness.

When we woke up the next evening, we heard a knock on our door.

Patrick answered, and Andrew walked into the room. He studied us and frowned. We were dirty and bloody and wearing torn clothes thanks to our battle with Margaret.

"What happened?" he asked, appalled.

We told him everything that had transpired and where we'd left Margaret.

"Good lord," he said. "She had me fooled." He entered the secret room and returned a short time later. "She was awake—and unhappy. I put her back to sleep."

"Did you kick her in the face?" I asked. "Because that's what I had to do."

"No. I used magic." He lifted his foot. "These are new shoes." He shook his head. "I saw Milton's body. She did a real number on him. Without vampire blood, she's as weak as a kitten. She tried to convince me you two had kidnapped her and planned to drain her."

"Vampires don't do that," I said, irritated. "Where is she getting her information?"

"The Society," said Patrick. "Whatever that is."

"We know about the Society," said Andrew. "A group of vampire hunters that operated in the early 1900s. It went defunct in the seventies after the last members passed away." He looked at the floor. "Except for one, apparently. If she's the last of the Society, you won't need to worry about vampire hunters."

"We can handle vampire hunters," said Patrick.

"Of that, I have no doubt," said Andrew. "Are you sure you two want to make a go of it on this island?"

"More than ever," I said. "We will scrub it free of its nefarious past and build something new and bright and lovely here.

I won't hear another word about this place being cursed," I warned him. "Not from you. Not from anyone."

Andrew lifted his hands in a gesture of surrender. "Not a word from me."

"Is everyone else gone?" asked Patrick.

Andrew nodded. "The ferry works now. All you have to do is drive down and get on it. Patrick I'll be in touch with you about how you can acquire this property. We may need to work through the supernatural authorities because of everything that's happened here."

"I'm sure we can come to an arrangement," said Patrick. He took my hand and lifted it, brushing his mouth across my knuckles. "What Jessica wants Jessica gets."

What I wanted was a new beginning for my husband and I. And I wanted to create a haven for everyone who came to Willescane Island.

No more secrets.

No more lies.

No more tragedies.

From now on, this place would be all about peace and tranquility.

Right?

EPILOGUE

Six months later...
Patrick and I stood in the middle of Maine Street. Get it? *Maine* Street? Okay, maybe I was the only one that found that funny.

Our new town had one café, an herbal and magic store for those who practiced witchcraft or liked gourmet cooking, a space for a doctor's office and three other office spaces, and a chocolate shop. The biggest place on the street was the General Store, which was like our version of Wal-Mart. We wanted this island to be a sanctuary for both those who lived here and those who would come to visit the B&B in a safe atmosphere where everybody can be themselves—vampire, shifter, fairy, witch, or whatever.

"It's got that new town smell," I said. "Three more weeks until everything's finished. Then we can open the town and the bed-and-breakfast for business."

"What about Claire?" he asked. "Has she accepted our offer to be the town doctor?"

"Called me back this morning," she said. "She's in."

"Is she still in touch with Serena and Evan?"

"She is. Evan and Serena got married and are doing well. So is their daughter."

"Glad to hear it." Patrick hugged me. "I think Patsy will be here soon."

"Okay. Let's go to our new place."

We used our vampire magic to transport to the Stranger Inn—our renamed bed-and-breakfast retreat. We'd done a lot of work on the house itself. Everything was vampire proof— including special paint on the walls and blackout curtains in all the rooms. We'd also rebuilt the burned-down cottage and added two more.

Patsy Marchand, my friend and president of the Broken Heart Council, waited for us on the porch. I hugged her hard, and she laughed. "Man, you are spine-cracker, honey. Well, let me in already."

"Wow," said Patsy as she entered the inn. "This is amazing, y'all. I wish I could go hide away on an island. I've got three kids in college and one kid in high school and a whole lot of vampires on my ass all the time. Think I could hide out in one of those rooms upstairs?"

I laughed. "Of course. I won't tell anyone."

Patsy lifted a blonde brow. "Honey, you couldn't keep a secret if the world depended on it."

"Hey," I said. "I can, too."

"Uh-huh. Look, I can't stay long, but when you're ready, you know there is a lot of people from Broken Heart who will be here for the grand opening."

"I know."

Remember, how there were eight different vampire bloodlines, and each bloodline came with different powers? Patsy was part of the Amahte line, and she had the ability to raise zombies and talk to spirits. She saw ghosts all day long. I kinda wanted to ask her if the Willescanes, especially little Sophia, were still hanging around.

But I decided not to infringe on her time. At least not now.

Patsy dug into her oversized bag and pulled out a jar. When I looked into it I saw a tiny pixie I recognized.

"Oh my God," I said. "You kidnapped Flet."

"No. He's on loan from Simone and Brady. Turns out this little bug is allowed to give you one wish as a blessing for your new place." She grinned at me. "What do you say, Jess? You want to wish to eat again?"

"Yes!" I pumped my first. "We'll get a lot of undead business if they know they can eat real food here. And I'll be able to eat Godiva again. Patsy, you are the best!"

"Don't I know it." She uncapped the jar and Flet popped out. He shook his tiny wings and flew close to my face, his expression grumpy.

"I'm not just some wish-giving pixie, you know," he said. "I have other talents."

"Yeah," muttered Patsy, "a talent for getting into trouble."

Flet huffed. Then he rolled his hand toward me. "I can grant you a blessing, Jessica. What is your wish?"

"For everyone on this island to eat any and all the food they want."

He threw out his arms. "Granted!" He looked at Patsy. "Can we go home now?"

"Yep."

"Okay, kids. We're off." She gave me a hug and then squeezed on Patrick. "See you soon."

Patsy waved at us and then sparkled out of sight.

Not more than two minutes later, the inn's phone rang.

I looked at my husband. "Oh my gosh! Our first phone call." I picked up the phone and said, "Stranger Inn on Willescane Island. How may I help you?"

A man's deep voice said, "I would like to book the entire

place for the summer solstice. There will be twelve of us. All vampires."

We had plenty of space for a dozen undead. "Is this a family reunion," I asked, "or a corporate event?"

"Oh. Um. Let's call it a mental health retreat," he said. "My name is Dr. Cauldwell Baker and I specialize in vampire anger management. Is that all right? We'll be doing workshops and therapy sessions for our clients. It'll be me, my assistant, and ten of our patients."

"No problem," I said. I took down his information and got his credit card information. I hung up the phone. "Woohoo! We got our first booking," I said.

"Great," said Patrick. "Who?"

I grinned. "Twelve angry vampires."

Keep reading for an extended look at *Your Lycan or Mine?*

YOUR LYCAN OR MINE?

An Extended Sneak Peek

CHAPTER ONE

Las Vegas, Nevada

ASH KNEW SOMEONE was following her.

To get out of the stifling heat and suffocating quiet of the Soul Searchers office, she'd taken an evening walk. Her investigative partner, best friend, and pain-in-the-ass werewolf Sedrick "Nor" North had sashayed his drag queen self down to the Four Queens to flirt with the bartender.

Their office building wasn't far from the recently refurbished downtown. The shops on this particular street were closed, but the window displays and the wrought iron street lamps offered soft light. Well-trimmed trees sprouted from perfect dirt squares, which alternated with big pots of multi-colored flowers. Keeping non-indigenous plants alive in the desert took a lot of work—and water.

She stopped at a shop window, using its reflection to see who or what might be trailing her. Moments passed, and no one appeared around the corner. It seemed as though she was alone. Ash cut her eyes to the right and then to the left. Nothing stirred, not even the Las Vegas wind.

A shiver of foreboding made goosebumps rise on her flesh. Everything was so still. Quiet. The air felt heavy, as though storm brewed just beyond the horizon. She couldn't shake the feeling that she was standing helplessly in that awful silence before the thunder roared and the sky cracked open.

Jittery, Ash turned away from the shop. Forget waiting. She'd draw out the one following her.

She stretched her fingers and cracked her neck as she casually continued her stroll. She was never without weapons. She always carried poisoned knives on the sides of her boots. Every pair she owned had compartments to store the specially made blades. Her Sig Sauer .45 rested in her shoulder holster.

Potent soul-shifter magic coursed through her the same way the blood did in her veins though she tried not to use her magic. Magic was energy and using it drained her faster than relying on fists and feet to combat a foe. She was more likely to throw a punch than she was to delve into her supernatural gifts.

Up ahead, she saw the entrance to an alleyway that she knew led to a dead end. If she could draw in her unwanted companion, she'd have the advantage. Her stalker wouldn't have anywhere to go.

As she passed the alley's entrance, she swerved into it and ran as fast as she could to the very back. She positioned herself against the brick wall next to a foul-smelling Dumpster, and kept her gaze ahead, waiting.

"C'mon," she muttered. "Show yourself."

She didn't hear footsteps or the rough breathing of someone running. No, she felt the oppressive presence slither into the alleyway. The effluvium was so thick that it nearly suffocated her.

"Ash the Destroyer," hissed a gravelly voice. "Thy death is upon you."

"Says you." Her denial croaked out in a ragged whisper. A force she could not see grabbed her throat and pushed her against the wall.

She kicked and punched, but met no resistance. The thing attacking her had no form. She smelled the sulfur, though, and knew the thing trying to strangle her was demonic. The edges of her vision darkened and she gasped for breath. Her only option was magic. She drew on her power and released it through her fingertips. The blue and white energy struck the invisible foe like a lightning bolt. The creature screamed but did not let go. The pressure on her throat increased.

"Close your eyes," yelled a male voice.

She squeezed her eyes shut. She felt an explosion of powerful energy. The miasma attacking her shattered, and a frustrated screech echoed as the evil released its hold on her.

Ash gulped air and rubbed her raw throat. Her heart pounded furiously, and her hands shook uncontrollably.

"Natasha," said a deep, silky voice. She looked up at the man approaching her. He was dressed in a tailored pinstriped Armani suit. His dark hair was short and cut corporate style. He had the sharp, good looks of a GQ model and the arrogant attitude of an alpha male. His dark eyes reminded her of polished amber.

"Who the hell are you?" she managed in a cracked voice.

"I'm the guy who just saved your life." He looked her over with one eyebrow cocked. "I'm disappointed. I expected more from the infamous soul shifter."

"Yeah?" Unnerved by her brush with the demon and irritated with his tone of voice, she kicked him in the kneecap.

He stumbled, and she punched him hard in the solar plexus. He flew backward.

He lay stunned on the ground. She took out her Sig and aimed it at the stranger. "I asked you a question, asshole."

He grinned, not intimated by her at all. "I'm Jarod Dante. Your new boss."

"I don't have a boss." Ash wracked her brain. Why did the name Jarod Dante seem so familiar?

"I know Damian and Kelsey," he said, as though he'd guessed at her thoughts. "I'm a friend to Broken Heart."

Ash remembered now. Jarod was a therianthrope who'd hoped to mate with Kelsey, a Changeling. But Damian, king of the lycanthropes, had accidentally turned her into a werewolf, and they fell in love. Jarod had been left out in the cold, and then he disappeared. Why the hell would he show up to save her and outrageously claim he was her boss?

She watched Jarod climb to his feet. He crossed his arms, which tightened the expensive material and showed off impressive biceps. He made her nerve endings buzz with awareness, and she didn't fucking like it.

"The balance between Light and Dark is teetering," he said. "The Convocation has been resurrected to restore the balance."

The Convocation reborn? *No, thank you.* "Wait. *You're* part of the Convocation?"

"Yes." He shrugged. "I needed something to do with my time."

Jarod was playing his cards close to the vest. Didn't matter. She had no hope that anything would be different from the original incarnation. "You tell the new Convocation to kiss my ass."

"Tempting offer," he said. "It is a delectable ass."

His comment stunned her into silence. Reeling from the

unwelcome attraction to the man, she attempted to stride past him.

Jarod grabbed her arm and spun her around to face him. His expression became grave. "Why do you think a demon tried to kill you?"

She yanked her arm from his grip. "Everyone tries to kill me."

"The Vedere psychics have issued a prophecy."

Ash frowned. "About me?"

"About Lilith." He paused. "And you."

"I can't wait to hear this."

"Lilith returns, the world burns. The soul shifter is the only key that ensures the demon is never free."

"Why do they make everything rhyme? It's hard to take their prophecies seriously." She narrowed her gaze. "Is this a job for Convocation? Because the answer is a big, fat no."

"The Convocation isn't asking you for anything, Natasha. Fate is the one coming for you." His gaze gentled and his tone softened. "Remember, when the time comes, you must begin where the first sacrifices were made."

Jarod disappeared. No sparkles. No smoke. Not even a good-bye. He just wasn't there anymore.

Rattled by the demon attack, Jarod Dante's appearance, and the news about Lilith, Ash pushed her hands into the pockets of her pink leather jacket and hurried back to the office.

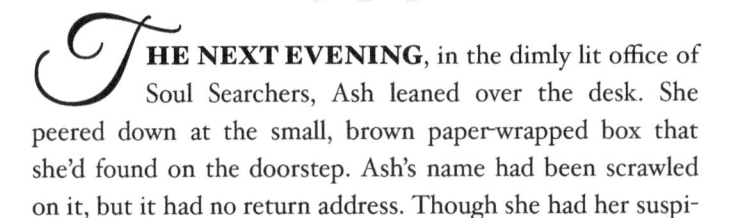

THE NEXT EVENING, in the dimly lit office of Soul Searchers, Ash leaned over the desk. She peered down at the small, brown paper-wrapped box that she'd found on the doorstep. Ash's name had been scrawled on it, but it had no return address. Though she had her suspicions, she hadn't found any clues about where it had come from or who had dropped it off.

"Did you get me a present?" asked Nor, looking fabulous in his electric-blue mini skirt and white blouse. His stilettos were the same eye-popping color as the skirt. He'd gone for a blond pageboy wig. A faux diamond dotted his cheek. His lips were cherry red, his eye shadow glittery blue.

"Only waitresses in roadside diners and hookers past their prime wear that color of eye shadow," groused Ash.

"Jealous much." Nor blinked at her, oblivious to Ash's worry, and gave her the full effect of his false lashes.

"Did you kill a couple of spiders and glue them to your eyes?"

"Ouch." He put a hand to his heart in mock pain. "Remember who taught you how to deliver the throat-punch-groin-kick combo. These heels can draw blood."

He joined Ash at the desk and looked at the box. "Money?" Nor's voice was hopeful. "Come on, large wad of cash!"

"Bomb," suggested Ash cynically.

He poked it. "It's not ticking."

"Bombs don't have to tick." She batted his hand away. "Maybe it's biological. If we open it ... poof ... poison sprays in our faces." She grabbed her throat and made choking noises.

"You're horrifyingly jaded."

"Only about mysterious packages."

"I say we open it." Nor scooped up the box and shook it like a maraca.

Ash reached for the package, but Nor was nearly a foot taller than her. He held it above her head and laughed.

"You don't know what's in there!" she screeched.

"I will in a minuuuuute." He danced backward, and she aimed her boot at his shin. He darted to the left. "Hey! Don't kick me! I bruise easily, and you'll ruin my perfect legs."

"Okay, okay. You do have pretty good legs." Besides, the

damned bomb would've gone off by now. "But you're still a dumbass."

"As long as it's cute, I don't care about the intelligence level of my ass." He tore off the paper, throwing it into a nearby trashcan, and then removed the lid. He stared at the contents, frowning.

"What is it?" she asked.

"Statuary. God, I hate knick-knacks. Especially broken knick-knacks." He handed her the box. "Do you think it's worth anything? Maybe we could sell it to a pawnshop and go to the Four Queens for drinks. It's half-price night at the bar."

"It's always half-price night for you. The bartender wants to get under your skirt."

Nor chuckled. "He's so yummy that I'd let him. Too bad he's not the type to enjoy what's under there."

"The way he flirts with you," she said, looking him up and down, "means he's definitely into what's under there."

The tall, leggy werewolf batted his eyelashes again.

Ash shook her head, hiding a smile, as she took out the statue: a headless lion the color of mustard and formed out of cheap clay. Foreboding washed over her and Ash's stomach clenched. Her adopted parents had an odd statue like this one. Dad was a professor of ancient cultures, and he often traveled the world in pursuit of knowledge. He had a lot of weird objects. The statue had always appeared like a cheap knock-off to her. The garish colors and the rough clay parts looked like the efforts of a kindergartner.

"I've seen this before," she said. "It's supposed to have an owl head and a snake necklace."

"As if it's not gaudy enough," said Nor, horrified.

She tapped the statue. "I think this means we have a job."

"Funny, I don't see a client or his deposit." He looked at Ash. "Remember our new philosophy? You can't pay; we don't play. Cough up the dough or we won't go. If a monster caught is what you wish then you better pass the money dish."

Ash grimaced. "I can't believe you remembered those awful mottos we cooked up. We were drunk, Nor."

"Doesn't matter. We're running a business, not a charity."

"Jeez! Who's cynical now?" She put the statue on the desk and picked up the box. "You know how this works. It's my calling. It's who I am, not just what I do."

"Penance for the souls you devour?" Nor sighed. "Fine. But being noble doesn't pay the bills or put food in our bellies."

"Or buy booze."

"That too."

"We'll try to scare up a paying gig," said Ash. She removed the tissue paper and shook it out. A square-cut piece of parchment floated free. She snatched it and read the note out loud. "If the portal opens to Lilith's hell, only the eater of souls can break the spell. Find three sacrifices from the soul shifter's heart, 'tis the only way to keep out the dark."

"A threat has been issued in badly written rhyme." Nor eyed the headless lion warily. "Eater of souls is a little dramatic."

"The Vedere psychics and their goddamned prophecies. They love being mysterious and secretive." Ash wondered if Jarod had put the Convocation up to this. She couldn't be sure. The statue might be from the Vederes. Ash sighed, leaning back in her chair. She hadn't told Nor about Jarod yet. She didn't want to freak out her friend. Or, to be honest, acknowledge she had the hots for a dude. Nor would spot her hormone fluctuations from a mile away.

"Why is this shit never easy?" asked Nor.

"If it were easy, everyone would do it." Ash stared at the headless lion. *Remember, when the time comes, you must begin where the first sacrifices were made.* She understood now what

Jarod meant. She had to go home to Tulsa. Her heart turned over in her chest. "Before we save the world, I need a drink."

Nor stood up and straightened his dress. "Amen, sistah." He looked at Ash, who sat in the office chair with her feet propped on the desk. He leaned a hip against it, frowning. "We deal with demons all the time. This is Las Vegas. Those scaly bastards love it here. You can practically drown in all the sin. We got this, babycakes."

"Yeah. End of the world stuff. No big deal."

Nor sighed. "Can we get *anyone* to pay us for this gig?"

"What? Saving the entire planet isn't enough for you?"

"The electric company doesn't take global gratitude as payment for a bill that's three months overdue."

The lights flickered. Ash and Nor looked at each other, eyes wide. Then the whole office went dark. The buzzing of the electric appliances, from the computer to the coffee maker, silenced.

In the quiet darkness, Nor said, "Told you so."

CHAPTER TWO

Three days later
Tulsa, Oklahoma

"I HEARD YOU killed the last dragon," said the drunk.

Ugh. Was that the only thing that impressed parakind these days? Technically, Ash hadn't taken down Synd by herself. The dark mage was dead, except his soul had been missing. And not because Ash took it. It was gone before she killed him. P.S. She happened to know there were a few dragons left and living happily in Broken Heart, Oklahoma, even though the world thought them gone forever.

"You don't look like much. I could take you."

Ash didn't bother looking up from her drink. She'd been imbibing liquid courage to visit where her childhood died. Where everything died. She did not want to go to a place she'd only revisited in nightmares.

To top off her shitty mood, the moron standing next to her table was either an asshole looking to impress other assholes or he was suicidal. He was certainly three sheets to the wind. At the table behind him, his buddies nudged each other, grinning widely.

Cripes.

The bar was small, dark, and seedy. It smelled like smoke and piss. The vinyl chairs were all duct-taped. The jukebox was broken, so the only noise was chattering voices peppered with laughter. Ash liked it here because the parakind patrons kept to themselves. Most people and creatures knew to leave her alone. Those who didn't end up with broken limbs.

Or worse.

Ash sipped her drink. Idly, she wondered how long the guy's patience would hold. Would he let his testosterone get the better of him? She hoped so. Ash hadn't punched anyone in a couple of days.

"Hey. I'm talking to you," the jerk said, his words slurred.

Ash rolled her eyes. She itched to pull out a dagger and jab it in his temple. Instead, she picked up her drink and finished it off.

Seconds later, Nor returned to the table with two rye whiskeys. His fingernails were painted neon pink, which matched his dress, heels, and wig. His make-up, as usual, was perfect. He was sexy as a man or a woman. His werewolf form wasn't bad, either.

Big, Tall, and Dumb sneered at Nor as he sat down. He crossed his legs and sipped his rye. He looked at Ash. "New beaux?"

"You know me, Nor. Got to beat 'em off with a stick."

"You wanna fight me? I'll fry your ass." The man reached down and grabbed her shoulder.

Ash looked up and met his gaze.

"Shit!" He let go and reared back. "They said you had a..." He trailed off, staring at her.

Diamond gaze. She'd heard it before. The night of her awakening, her eyes had turned such a light gray that they sometimes appeared translucent so that her pupils looked like black dots in orbs of white. It disturbed people—and giving 'em the heebie-jeebies often worked to her advantage.

She looked him over. Tall, buff, dressed in jeans and a biker jacket (idiot), he was a clone of every other blustering paranormal jerk who'd tried to make their bones by kicking her ass.

It never ended well.

For them.

"I ain't scared," he said, regaining his composure. He looked over his shoulder and apparently got a boost of confidence from his jeering friends.

"Go away."

"You saying I'm too tough for you?"

Nor laughed. "Oh, honey. You're adorable."

This was not the reaction the inebriated bully expected. He frowned. "Don't laugh at me, bitch."

Nor bared his teeth and let out a low growl.

Oh, for fuck's sake! This guy had a terminal case of stupidity. Ash looked at her half-finished drink, mourning its loss as she stood up. "Let's get out of here, Nor. I'm bored." She put a twenty on the table. Nor tossed the rest of his drink down the hatch and regally rose to his six and a half feet. With heels, he was six foot eight.

She plucked her pink leather jacket from the back of the chair. Ash hated to be a cliché—an assassin who strode around in leather, but hell, she loved her tailored jacket. Not only was it stylish, but it also had useful magical properties.

"You running away?" Stupid yelled. "That's right. You ain't shit."

Ash turned, pointed at him and released a tiny fraction of her power. Blue and white lights danced around her fingertip. "If you want to keep your soul, asshole, walk away."

The man's eyes widened.

Ash lifted an eyebrow and flicked the magic at him.

He yelped and turned, stumbling back toward his now silent friends.

Nor looped his arm through Ash's. "Well, that was fun."

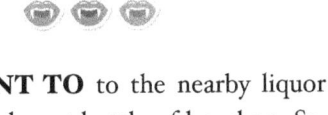

◆ ◆ ◆

*N*OR WENT TO to the nearby liquor store to pick up a decent bottle of bourbon. So, Ash had walked to the motel by herself. Since the bar shared the same parking lot, it only took about five minutes to reach the outdoor staircase that led to the second floor. She took the steps two at a time, rusted metal creaking in protest.

This joint was so ancient and so broken down that the owners hadn't bothered switching to a card-key system. She liked the old-fashioned brass key rattling in the lock.

A swish of magical energy warned her she was no longer alone.

She leaned her forehead against the door. Paint flaked off and drifted to the concrete. "I'm so not in the mood to kill you."

"I'm not in the mood to die."

Ash looked up. Jarod leaned against the concrete wall, looking at her, his dark eyes hiding his secrets.

But not his desires.

Ash unlocked the door and swung it open. "Go away." She went into the room and flicked on the light. It cast a dim, yellow glow from the single bulb dangling from the ceiling.

The room didn't boast any amenities. Hell, not even the antiquated television sitting on the dresser worked. The twin beds were hard as rocks. The chair in the corner had stuffing popping out of several tears.

"Wow. What did you ask for? The hobo special?"

"I prefer low key." Ash took off her jacket and tossed it onto the bed.

Jarod's gaze wandered over her black, skin-tight pants tucked into sturdy black boots and her pink tank top. His lazy examination sent electric shivers across her skin.

"I recognize Bernie's work. Not many people get to wear his creations." His gaze flicked to the jacket. "Did he make that, too?"

Ash shrugged. Jarod had a keen eye. Her friend and literal fashion wizard Bernie made all of Ash's clothes. He knew how to make magical materials that wouldn't cut, burn, tear, or restrict. The jacket was one-of-a-kind. It had a dozen pockets. She could hide anything, huge or tiny, in them. They all offered endless storage, and the cloth stretched to accommodate just about any object.

Ash crawled on the bed, leaning against the cheap headboard and stretched out her legs. "What do you want?"

"I'm checking on you."

"You mean you're checking to see if I'm doing what the Convocation wants."

"Convocation 2.0 isn't so bad," he said as he sat on the bed opposite of hers.

Most parakind were terrified of her. Nobody who liked living was completely unafraid of Ash. It was one thing to die. It was quite another to have your essence stolen and stored inside a being with the ability to assume your form. For creatures unfortunate enough to be absorbed by Ash, there was no afterlife.

Ash felt a flicker of guilt, but it did no good to feel sorry about what came naturally to her. Working for the Convocation meant maintaining the balance both ways. Whoever the Convocation marked, she'd taken their souls—good or bad.

She didn't do that anymore.

Most people born on the Earth got to choose what kind

of lives they had. They went to school or traveled or took jobs and raised families. They worried about things like love and happiness and loss and sorrow. But for Ash, there was never a choice. Sometimes, you were born into your destiny.

She couldn't change the fact that she was a soul shifter. But only she got to decide how to live her life. Ash would never have a family or a husband or a nine-to-five job. She would never be normal, never be anything other than what she'd been born. But how she used her gift was her choice and hers alone.

Jarod seemed content in the silence and in a weak moment, she allowed herself to think that he was kinda cute.

The door flew open. Nor posed in the doorway, holding a liter of Buffalo Trace in one hand and a bag of ice in the other. "I'm ba-ack!" He looked at Jarod and grinned, obviously delighted. "Ooooh. You brought me eye candy." He lifted the bourbon. "Drink?"

"None for me, thanks," said Jarod.

Ash held up two fingers. "I'll have a double."

Nor strode to the dresser and unwrapped the flimsy plastic cups provided by the motel. A couple minutes later, he handed a cup to Ash. "It's a triple." He took his drink and sat next to the soul shifter. "Who's the yum?" Nor asked. He crossed his legs and looked at Jarod critically. Then he sighed dramatically. "Straight. Too bad." He waved his manicured hand around. "I guess you can have him, Ash."

"Gee, thanks."

Nor's eyes widened and he gasped. "Is he a client? Oh please, please, please let him be a paying client!"

"He's not a client," said Ash. "Unfortunately, he's a minion of the new Convocation."

"I'm not a minion," protested Jarod.

"The Convocation?" Nor pointed at Jarod. "We don't like

those uppity bitches. You're not here to recruit my BFF again, are you?"

"No." He turned his gaze to Ash. "I know you received the lion's body."

"Because you sent it."

He shook his head. "Not me. But I do know it's a statue dedicated to Lilith. Lion body. Owl head. Snake necklace."

"Do you know about the bad poetry we received with the headless beast?" Nor sipped his bourbon. "Apparently, my girl is the only one who can keep the demon Lilith from destroying the world."

"I know about the prophecy." He stared at Nor until the werewolf popped up and said, "I need more...um, ice. I'll be back."

Nor left the room, and Ash looked at Jarod. "Subtle."

Jarod moved to her bed and put her booted feet on his lap. She eyed him suspiciously. He pulled off her boots and her thick socks, and then pushed up her pant legs and starting massaging her feet and calves.

"What are you doing?" Whoa. His strong, warm hands against her tension-filled muscles felt so good. The stiffness of stress started to drain and contentment curled in her belly. It would be stupid to give up a free massage just because she didn't want to be attracted to Jarod. Or so she told herself. She enjoyed his touch, and her body hummed with anticipation.

"You want me," he said.

"Said the arrogant therianthrope."

He laughed. "I want you, too."

Why lie? "Yeah, okay. We got sparks, but so what?"

He stopped his excellent massage. She bit back a protest. He stood up and offered her his hand. She looked up at him, feeling lazy. One eyebrow winged upward. He wiggled his fingers and with a huge sigh, she clasped his hand and he pulled her to her feet. He plucked the cup from her grasp and placed it on the rickety nightstand.

"Natasha."

"My name is Ash."

"Not to me."

"Whatever." Ash's gaze dipped to his luscious mouth. Oh, she shouldn't be looking at him like that. And her heart shouldn't thunder in her chest. And she shouldn't be even the teeniest bit attracted to him.

"You know, most humans aren't as stubborn as you are."

"I'm not human."

"But you are a woman," he said, leaning down to nuzzle her neck. "And I'm a man."

"I'm so glad we've clarified our genders." Ash figured she should pull out of his embrace. Then punch him for daring to assume she'd even consider sleeping with him. It had been a while since she'd been with anyone. Rare was the man who kept her interest. Besides, she tended to terrify most red-blooded males.

Somehow, she knew that Jarod would be the kind of man she'd never get enough of ... the kind of guy that would never want to tame her, but could match her in every way. Oh, shit. She was in trouble with a capital T.

"I see your dilemma," he said, lifting his head to stare at her. "You can't decide if you want to kill me ... or kiss me."

"Kill you," she whispered. "Definitely."

His lips pulled into a wicked grin. "You could try."

"Maybe I will," Ash said breathlessly, her lips within tantalizing reach of Jarod's.

The first brush of his lips was electric.

Sparks? More like nuclear explosion. Her whole body went molten. She gave in to her lust, returning his kiss with fervor, drawing him closer, wanting more.

Ash broke the kiss. She didn't let go of him—she might collapse if she did. "What are we doing?"

"Having fun. Are you going to say I caught you in a weak moment?"

A whirlwind of emotions claimed her. She tried to sort through them and pick one to flail him with.

"You regret it. You never want it to happen again. I should take a flying leap." His fingers stroked the small of her back in contradiction to his words.

"Do you need me to participate in the conversation?" asked Ash, the chill of her reluctance thawing with his every touch. He brushed a tender kiss on her lips. She melted completely. This was so not like her. She blew out a breath. "We shouldn't do this ... whatever this is."

Jarod pulled back and looked at her. "We're perfect for each other, you know."

"That's only possible if you don't have a soul. When I get the munchies somebody dies."

"You can't take my soul, Natasha. I'm a therianthrope."

She frowned. "So?"

"I'm the last of my kind, just as you are. I'm the one creature on this earth whose soul will never be yours."

"How is that possible?"

"Turns out therianthropes and soul-shifters have a mating history. Did you know soul shifters were only female?"

Ash reared back. "What?"

"Soul shifters needed mates immune to their peculiar hunger."

"Therianthropes."

"Yes. It makes sense. You and I both can change forms. Granted my way is easier because my DNA is malleable."

"So now we're destined mates?" She pulled away and put distance between them. "One kiss doesn't mean we're gonna get married."

Jarod laughed. "Relax, Natasha. I promise not to drag you down the aisle."

Ash noticed he didn't deny his belief that they were mates. She didn't know what stunned her more: The fact he'd suggested it or the fact she didn't hate the idea.

"I have work to do." Flustered, she grabbed her boots off the floor and started to yank them on.

"Are you sure you want to face the past alone?"

She didn't bother asking how he knew why she was here. After all, he'd sent her this direction with all that talk of remembering where the first sacrifices were made.

"You really think my parents' deaths are because of Lilith? That she knew I was the one who could keep her bound?"

"Yes," he murmured. "They had you, the statue, and the prophecy. The problem is that Lilith struck before they could prepare you. And then the Convocation scooped you up."

"Yeah. And what a joy that turned out to be."

Jarod stepped closer to her and cupped her face. His concerned gaze met hers. "Do you need back-up?"

"I have to do this alone," said Ash. "I'm not even taking Nor."

"If you need me..." He trailed off, his gaze filled with genuine concern.

"Yeah," she said, uncomfortable with his obvious worry for her. "Thanks."

CHAPTER THREE

Marietta, Ohio

CLAIRE GLASS WANDERED among the garage-sale treasures. She touched votive candles, potholders, Matchbox cars, and a cookbook. Her fingertips relayed the differences in textures. Smooth. Soft. Bumpy. She could see the sizes and shapes of the items.

The colors were missing.

Gray permeated her once vibrant world. How she longed to see a red rose, a blue sky, and a green Starbuck's logo. Had it been only a year since every happy thing in her life had been stolen? The man she loved. The wedding they'd planned. The new promotion she'd gotten. *Hmph*. Difficult to be an interior designer without the ability to see color. Even their dream house, which they'd only moved into the week before the accident, had been taken.

Without Henry or her job, she hadn't been able to afford the mortgage payments. Now, she lived in a tiny apartment trying to make ends meet with disability and Henry's life insurance money.

When she'd come out of the coma, the doctors told her that her cerebral cortex had been damaged. Cerebral achromatopsia was the result. She was lucky to be alive and luckier still that only her limited vision was the price paid for the same wreck that took Henry's life.

Snap out of it, girl. Pity parties are so lame. Claire rounded the corner of the table and looked at the items displayed on a rickety bookshelf. Her fingers danced along an assortment of Precious Moments figurines. She knew why she was so damned mopey. Today would've been her first wedding anniversary. Had Henry lived, they would be celebrating, maybe even taking the first step toward starting a family.

Her gaze swept the driveway, looking at the careless displays of toys, shoes, and tools. *What the—*

Heart thumping, Claire leaned down and reached into the cardboard box labeled "Miscellaneous - 25¢ each." The owl head was as wide as her hand and looked familiar. She could see groves in the neck where the head connected to another piece. It was a shame it wasn't intact, but the broken statuary was still extraordinary.

She saw its color.

The owl head was a brilliant red. Claire looked around. If she could see color again, maybe her vision was getting better. What did doctors know? Miracles happened every day.

As her eager gaze bounced around the neighborhood -- staring at cars, at people, at lawns, she saw the dreary grayness she always did. She looked at the owl head again. For some odd reason, she only saw this object in color.

She stared at it, searching her memory. Where had she seen this before?

Natasha's house.

Her best friend in junior high, Natasha Nelson, had shown her the odd statue during a sleepover. It had an owl head, a lion body, and a snake necklace. Natasha's father studied ancient cultures and supposedly he'd found it on some kind of dig in Israel.

Just before Claire's sophomore year in high school, her father took a new job, and the family moved to Ohio. She hadn't seen or heard from Natasha in years.

She chuckled. This could not possibly be the same owl's head.

What did it matter? She had proof that her vision was healing. Grinning like a lottery winner, Claire dug out her wallet and extracted a quarter.

Finding this little guy was like getting a message from Henry. *I'll always take care of you, Claire. Always.* That had been the promise he reiterated every day of their lives together. It felt like the statue was his gift to her; a reminder that he was still keeping that promise.

Tulsa, Oklahoma

AFTER SEEING NOR off at the airport, Ash had gone straight to her old neighborhood. She pulled into the gravel driveway and let the rental car idle. The house was abandoned, the yard unkempt, and the metal fence rusted and broken. Honeysuckle bushes were thick around the listing gate. In the backyard, weeds poked up through the high grass. Somewhere in that mess were the remains of her terrier's doghouse.

Her gaze wandered over the dilapidated house. The Convocation had purchased it and given it to her. She'd let the place fall to rot and ruin because the idea of coming back sent panic crashing through her.

Were the answers to stopping Lilith actually in there? And how could her adopted parents' murders be related to what was happening now?

She felt frozen to the spot. Here was where her life had ended. A rebellious sixteen-year-old, she'd snuck out to go to a party and returned home to find her family murdered.

Ash tasted bile at the back of her throat. She'd never been back to Tulsa since the tragic loss of her family, much less this neighborhood. The only time she even thought about Oklahoma was when she popped into Broken Heart.

That awful night when she lost her parents and the Convocation rescued her, she was taken from the human world and thrust into the paranormal one. She wasn't allowed to do anything but train. Weapons. Martial arts. Magic rites. Learning how to kick ass had given her focus, a way to work out her grief and her rage. Her first jobs had short leashes held by iron-fisted chaperones. After a while, the Convocation trusted her to go into the world, to do her job, on her own.

Ash shut off the car's engine and shoved the passenger door open. What had she hoped to find here? Answers? Redemption? Hope?

She rounded the front of the car and walked to the gate. It was falling off its hinges. Honeysuckle wound through metal loops, reaching toward her like victims reciting last prayers. The sweet scent of the flowers made her nauseous. Staring at them, she drifted back to that night so long ago...

The sweet scent of honeysuckle wafted from the vines entwining the metal fence. She leaned down and tugged off a yellow blossom. Gently she pinched the stamen and withdrew it, licking away the pearl of nectar on its end.

Her mother had taught her how to do that.

Guilt crimped her stomach. She looked at the desecrated flower and wished she hadn't plucked it, hadn't stolen its honey. The yellow petals were already browning and curling inward. Sighing, she tossed it to the ground.

"That house is haunted."

Ash whirled around whipping out her hip daggers. The poisoned tips of the blades hovered above the head of the one who'd crept up on her.

"Are those real?" The little girl's sky-blue eyes were as wide as saucers. "Can I touch one?"

"No." Ash slid the daggers into their holsters. "Don't you know that sneaking up on people can get you killed?"

"It hasn't yet." The girl was dressed in overalls and a yellow shirt. Her feet were bare. Her brown hair was a rat's nest with twigs sticking out of it. The overalls were dirty, too. Cobwebs stuck to her shoulders. "You gonna buy that house?"

"No." Ash looked her over speculatively. "What were you doing in there?"

"I'm not allowed inside."

It wasn't a denial. Well, goddamn. Ash was trying to work up the nerve to go inside the home she'd lived in for nearly sixteen years and this little sprite had explored it already. She made Ash feel like a coward.

"I bet you're not afraid of anything," said the girl.

"You'd lose that bet." Ash stuck out her hand. "Call me Ash."

"That's a weird name." She grabbed Ash's hand and pumped it. "Margaret Lynne Huntson."

Huntson? Looked like her past knew she was arriving and had thrown a party. "Is your father named Rick?"

"Yes. Do you know him?"

He almost kissed me. I almost fell in love with him. "No," she said. "I don't know your daddy. I'm a good guesser."

Margaret Lynne Huntson considered this possibility. Then she peered up Ash suspiciously. "What's my mommy's name?"

"Maggie?"

Margaret's gaze re-evaluated Ash's intelligence. "You're not a good guesser. You're just lucky."

Wrong again, kid.

"My birthday was yesterday," confided Margaret. "I'm officially eight years old."

"That's fascinating. Hey! Isn't it almost dinner time?"

"Nope. You look like my Rock n' Roll Barbie, only she has better hair."

"Oh, yeah? Have you looked in the mirror lately?"

But Margaret was bored with hairstyle insults. She chewed on her thumb. "What're you doing here?"

Oh, for the love of humanity. Why couldn't this kid just go away? "Ever hear of the Ghostbusters?"

"Ghostbusters don't wear pink."

"I do." Ash squatted down and got eye-to-eye with her. "Do you know why this house is haunted?"

The girl's eyes flickered. Once again, Ash felt like she was being judged. "Daddy says a girl lived here. Her name was Natasha. A bad man killed her parents and took her away." She tilted her head. Dirt was smeared under her chin. "Do you think he killed Natasha, too?"

"Yes," said Ash. "He did."

"No, he didn't." Her declaration startled Ash. "So, are you gonna talk to the ghost lady?"

"What lady?"

"She's in there. She calls me Tashie. I don't think she's mean," said Margaret. "Just sad." She ran to the fence and pulled off a honeysuckle blossom. "Hey, do you know how to get the honey?"

Ash's stomach squeezed. "Why don't you show me?"

"You just take this part out, very carefully." Margaret gently tugged the stamen out and showed it to Ash. "Then you lick it." Her little pink tongue darted across the fuzzy end. "Do you want to try?"

"Maybe later."

Margaret rolled her eyes. "That's what grown-ups say

when they mean no." She tossed the flower to the ground. "I gotta go home now."

Ash watched her run down the driveway and wondered how her bare feet could take the biting abuse of the gravel. She crossed the street and pivoted right, skipping down the sidewalk.

She was going in the direction of Rick's old house. Three blocks up, two blocks to the right, and one block left. Did he still live there? Or had he just moved into the same neighborhood? Oh, hell. Why did she care?

Her gaze caught the discarded flower. Then she looked at the house.

It was time to face her ghosts.

BROKEN HEART BOOKS

Broken Heart Paranormal Romances

#1 - I'm the Vampire, That's Why

#2 - Don't Talk Back to Your Vampire

#3 - Because Your Vampire Said So

#4 - Wait Till Your Vampire Gets Home

#5 - Over My Dead Body

#6 - Come Hell or High Water

#7 - Cross Your Heart

#8 - Must Love Lycans

#9 - Only Lycans Need Apply

#10 - Broken Heart Tails

#11 - Some Lycan Hot

#12 - You'll Understand When You're Dead

#13 - Lycan on the Edge

#14 - Your Lycan or Mine?

Lost Souls & Broken Hearts

A Broken Heart Paranormal Romance Spin-off

#1 - Amazing Grace

#2 - Peace in the Valley

#3 - How Great Thou Art

Broken Heart Paranormal Cozy Mysteries

#1 - Dirty Rotten Vampires (October 2018)

#2 - Twelve Angry Vampires (January 2019)

#3 - Citizen Vampire (April 2019)

#4 - The Vampire Connection (August 2019)

#5 - A Vampire in Paris (October 2019)

ROMANCES BY MICHELE BARDSLEY

Broken Heart Paranormal Romances

#1 - I'm the Vampire, That's Why

#2 - Don't Talk Back to Your Vampire

#3 - Because Your Vampire Said So

#4 - Wait Till Your Vampire Gets Home

#5 - Over My Dead Body

#6 - Come Hell or High Water

#7 - Cross Your Heart

#8 - Must Love Lycans

#9 - Only Lycans Need Apply

#10 - Broken Heart Tails

#11 - Some Lycan Hot

#12 - You'll Understand When You're Dead

#13 - Lycan on the Edge

#14 - Your Lycan or Mine?

Lost Souls & Broken Hearts

A Broken Heart Paranormal Romance Spin-off

#1 - Amazing Grace

#2 - Peace in the Valley

#3 - How Great Thou Art

Wizards of Nevermore Fantasy Romances

#1 - Never Again

#2 - Now or Never

The Pack Rules Shifter Romances

#1 - Alpha

#2 - Wolves

#3 - Bears

#4 - Dragons

#5 - Cats

Single Title Paranormal Romances

Holiday Bites

Blood Kiss

Cursed

Wired

Magical Acts

Tek

Single Title Contemporary Romances

Frisky Business

Mirrors Falls: Daddy in Training and Bride in Training

MYSTERIES BY MICHELE BARDSLEY

Violetta Graves Paranormal Mysteries - The Complete Series - Available Now!

#1 - In Good Spirits

#2 - A Spirited Defense

#3 - Getting in the Spirit

#4 - Plagued by Spirits

#5 - Free Spirit

Graves Detective Agency Cozy Mysteries

#1 - A Grave Mistake (December 2019)

#2 - One Foot in the Grave (April 2019)

#3 - Grave Robber (June 2019)

#4 - Take It to the Grave (October 2019)

#5 - Grave Stone (January 2020)

Broken Heart Paranormal Cozy Mysteries

#1 - Dirty Rotten Vampires (October 2018)

#2 - Twelve Angry Vampires (January 2019)

#3 - Citizen Vampire (April 2019)

#4 - The Vampire Connection (August 2019)

#5 - A Vampire in Paris (October 2019)

Garden Grove Witches of the Northwest

#1 - A Witch in Thyme (November 2018)

#2 - Stop and Spell the Roses (February 2019)

#3 - Every Witch Has Her Thorn (May 2019)

#4 - Spells Get Better With Sage (August 2019)

#5 - Witch Hazel Are You? (November 2019)

Antique Shop Cozy Mysteries

#1 - The Case of the Caretaker's Curios (December 2019)

#2 - The Case of the Ballerina's Bauble (March 2019)

#3 - The Case of the Tyrant's Treasure (July 2019)

#4 - The Case of the Actor's Artwork (September 2019)

#5 - The Case of the Widow's Watch (December 2019)

ABOUT THE AUTHOR

Michele Bardsley is a *New York Times* and *USA Today* bestselling author of paranormal fiction. When she's not writing tales of otherworldly adventures, she consumes chocolate, crochets hats, reads voraciously, and spends time with her Viking hubby and their fur babies.

Visit Michele's Website
http://www.michelebardsley.com

Subscribe to Michele's Newsletter
http://www.michelebardsleynewsletter.com

- facebook.com/MicheleBardsleyNovels
- bookbub.com/authors/michele-bardsley
- goodreads.com/michelebardsley
- amazon.com/author/michelebardsley